swinging at love

Suttonville
Sentinels

swinging at love

Suttonville
Sentinels

at love

KENDRA C. HIGHLEY

Entangled Publishing, LLC
2614 South Timberline Road
Suite 109
Fort Collins, CO 80525
Visit our website at www.entangledpublishing.com.

Crush is an imprint of Entangled Publishing, LLC.

Edited by Heather Howland
Cover design by April Martinez
Cover art from Shutterstock and Thinkstock

Manufactured in the United States of America

First Edition March 2017

For my dad,
who taught me to love both books and baseball

Chapter One

ALYSSA

There's a sound that can only be made by an aluminum bat striking a baseball. *Ting!* Alyssa couldn't help turning her head to figure out which hitter clocked that ball, but based on the cheers of the Little League team in cages two, three, and four, it had to be one of them. Twelve-year-olds, a whole pack of them. Swing Away hadn't been this busy in weeks.

Dad came over and leaned against the chain-link fence that divided the snack bar/observation area from the cages. "Came out of nowhere. They're here for that big tournament in Dallas. Next step toward the World Series."

Alyssa nodded absently. The kid in cage two was trash-talking his buddies. At that age, the trash talk was mostly gestures and the word "dumbass" repeated over and over again. When the ball shot out of the machine—low-grade changeup—he whiffed it. His friends doubled over laughing. The kid glared at them and tried again. This time a fastball, medium speed, zoomed over the plate. Nothing but air.

"He's anticipating it too much," she murmured. "Ahead of the ball."

Dad smiled, the skin at the corners of his eyes crinkling. "I still don't understand why you gave up softball. You were the best hitter in the league. Second best pitcher, too."

Three years, and he was still a little sad about it. "I know, but I love to dance more."

"Could've done both." Dad turned to watch the kid in cage two. Another whiff. "And paid for college with a softball scholarship at a big-name school."

Maybe, but somewhere along the way, she'd lost her love of playing. She still loved the game, but the politics, the dirty play, the bruises, the long weekends traveling to tourneys… They didn't add up. "I'll get an academic scholarship, and I don't need to go to a Division I school. Not for a business degree. I can go to community college the first few semesters."

"Well, we have a year to think about that." He winced as the kid missed another ball. "Think the machine is acting up?"

She shook her head. Two of the machines were out of order—Swing Away was slowly falling apart—but at least six of them were in good shape. "It's the kid. I'll be right back."

She let herself into the batting area, trying to ignore the bad nets, the creaky gates, and especially cage five, where the pitching machine sat broken and dormant. Those were things to worry about later. Instead, she went to cage two. "You're ahead of the ball. Slow it down a split second, and you'll have it."

The kid's chin jutted out. "I'm fine."

"Not really," she said, keeping her tone kind. "You're basically giving it a false start every time. Slow down."

"She's a girl, Scout," one of the kid's buddies said. "What would she know?"

Sighing, Alyssa picked up a bat from the collection

Swinging at Love

...ybe Dad was right, maybe she should've stuck with
...At least there, two sports bras would be just fine.

...uren flopped onto her bed, letting Alyssa have the
..., ratty armchair in the corner. "Faith says she'll work
...us at the studio Saturday. Give us tips on form."

Alyssa grinned. "You mean she's going to pry herself off
...e long enough to teach us? Those two, I swear. They're in
...ir own little orbit or something."

"Right? So cute, but almost disgusting. Anyway, the
...aseball team starts regional playoffs tomorrow, and will be
...racticing a lot, so she has time."

"Good enough." Alyssa dragged her binder out of her
backpack. "Might as well start this."

"Bleck. Faith's so lucky. I wish we were seniors and could
coast the rest of the semester, too." Lauren made a face. "I
really don't want another year of high school stuff."

Alyssa wagged a pencil at her. "We can make it through
five weeks."

"Then we'll dance all summer!" Lauren pumped a fist in
the air. "It's going to be great."

Alyssa forced a smile. It would be great...if she passed
her audition.

---

outside the cage. "Move."

"I paid for this round!" Scout protested.

"I'll give you a full round on the house in exchange. Now, let me show you something." Muttering to herself about how grateful she was she never babysat, Alyssa rolled her shoulders and swung a few times, remembering the rhythm. Ready, she went to the plate and squared up, waiting for the *clack* that came before the ball was launched.

It came—fastball, medium speed. She let the bat fly, putting her weight behind it.

Ting!

The ball sailed over the net into the pit in the middle, where it would be fed back to the machines. Ignoring the "whoa" and "wow" from the crowd, she eyed the pitching machine. Another clack—changeup.

TING!

The ball sailed *over* the pit and hit the cinderblock wall at the very back of the complex. Point made, Alyssa turned around and looked Scout straight in the eye. "Slow. Down."

"Yeah, okay!" He scrambled into the cage as she left. A minute later, his bat made contact.

"And my work here is done." She went back to the front side of the complex and stuck her head into her dad's office. "Do you need anything? I promised Lauren we could meet to work on our group project for history."

"Go on ahead." His smile was strained. "I need to do some paperwork, so I'll stay until close."

She wanted to ask how bad it was, but she couldn't bring herself to. If she didn't ask, she could keep believing everything was fine. "Okay. I'll be home in time for dinner."

He nodded absently, already staring at the pile of bills on his desk. Alyssa let herself out. It was after five, and that history project wasn't getting itself done. She needed the AP credit, and the test was in four weeks. The soft spring breeze, with a warm edge that hinted at the summer's coming heat, toyed with her hair, blowing tendrils across her face. She scraped them back impatiently, wishing—not for the last time—that her hair was both as smooth and as long as Lauren's, or even their friend Faith's. Her curls refused to stay in a ponytail, and ballerina buns were the stuff of nightmares, requiring a bottle of hair spray and a small country's worth of bobby pins.

Her well-used Honda groaned a little when she started it. "Come on, be a good car."

It rattled but drove without complaint once she got it rolling. The tires jounced across the gravel lot, past the Little League team's van, and out onto the four-lane state highway that led back into Suttonville. It wasn't a long drive, but it was farther out than the Top Sports complex three miles from the heart of town.

Alyssa drove by it on the way to Lauren's. Cars and trucks filled the lot, and when she stopped at a light, she could see dozens of people milling around the mini-golf course. Top Sports' batting cages were outside, unlike Swing Away's indoor facility, but they were well-lit and covered by an awning. Off to one side, a fully equipped driving range was full of golfers. Based on what she'd heard—because she'd never set foot inside—there was an indoor complex with basketball and racquetball courts to rent, along with a ten-lane bowling alley that boasted league action. Membership was available for the low, low price of seventy-nine bucks a month—families for $199. Based on the crowd, plenty of people were willing to pay their outrageous fee.

How can Swing Away even compete? Glaring straight ahead, Alyssa gunned the Honda as soon as the light changed. Two broken pitching machines, decrepit vending machines, torn nets, a gravel parking lot… None of that compared to slick, shiny Top Sports.

By the time she made it to Lauren's neighborhood of two-

story homes and perfect lawns, Al[…] epic proportions in her stomach. [—] her beloved Swing Away make it? B[…] Dad didn't tell her, she wasn't blind. S[…] backpack out of the car and went to Lau[…] mother had painted it peacock blue last su[…] total sense.

"Alyssa bear!" Mrs. Willet waved her in[…] was dressed in teal leggings and a yellow s[…] enough to blind. "I have cookies!"

Alyssa's stomach growled, but she shook […] "Thanks, but I'm good. Watching my diet, you know[…] "The auditions aren't for six weeks." Mrs. Will[…] "You girls are plenty skinny."

"Mom." Lauren appeared at the upstairs banister. [—] fine."

Mrs. Willet shrugged. "All right, then. I'll be in the kitch[…] if you need me."

As soon as her back was turned, Lauren shook her head, […] chuckling. "She means well."

"And I'd give anything for a cookie, but the academy […] looks at *everything* and I'd rather not show off a muffin top." Alyssa climbed the stairs. "Maybe that's why I'm pissy. Living on fourteen hundred calories while dancing my butt off is making me cranky."

Lauren led her to her bedroom, wisely not saying anything. She was one of those naturally thin girls who could eat the world and still look like a sparrow in a size four. Madame Schuler at the studio called her figure the "ideal ballerina body." Alyssa could only imitate it by dieting and sucking everything in. She had an athlete's body—strong, flexible, and surefooted, but the Dallas Ballet Conservatory wanted waifish primas rather than girls who could leap higher than the rest. And D-cup breasts were definitely not on that list.

Chapter Two

Coach waved toward the batter's box. "Murrell, you're up."

Tristan stood and grabbed a bat. He started out of the dugout as Kyle Sawyer trotted down the steps, having just nailed four of seven pitches. "Show off."

Kyle laughed. "Talent."

Tristan couldn't argue with that. Kyle always played like his hair was on fire, but now that he was dating Faith, his game had improved to pro levels. The teams they were playing in the playoffs wouldn't know what hit them. Not that Tristan was any slouch. As soon as Kyle graduated, the Suttonville Sentinels would be *his* team.

Tristan trotted to the batter's box and swung his bat a few times, then posted up for the pitcher to throw to him. Dylan gave him a cocky grin. "Here for some punishment?"

"After what Sawyer just did to you? I'm here to clean up your mess." Tristan grinned and waggled his bat. "Bring it."

The first pitch was high and outside. "Ball!"

"Oh, come on!" Dylan glared at him and wound up again.

A nice, fat fastball hurtled toward Tristan. Yeah, this one was a grapefruit.

He swung, hard.

The ball sailed by him.

"Strike!" Dylan called, his grin returning. "Oh, I'm sorry… Were you planning to *hit* that?"

Tristan stared at the catcher, trying to unstick his brain from the miss. How did he not hit that? It should've been a homer, dead-center field. Instead, he'd whiffed it like a third grader.

"Enough with the trash talk, Dennings," Coach barked from the dugout. "How about a changeup?"

Tristan tightened his grip on the bat. Everyone missed sometimes. When a three hundred batting average was considered good, one out of three wasn't bad, and Tristan had a three twenty average. He'd hit the next one, no problem.

Except…he didn't. Out of seven pitches, he only clipped one foul. Tristan glared at his bat in betrayal. The first round of regional playoffs started tomorrow night. He couldn't go into a slump *now*.

"Shake it off." Kyle whacked him on the shoulder when he went back to the dugout. "Look at it this way—you got the bad ones out of the way. Now you'll be red hot."

"I guess." Tristan dropped his bat into his equipment bag.

"Hey, don't overthink it," Kyle said. "The more you stress, the worse it'll get. Let the mojo flow."

Tristan rolled his eyes. If you looked up mojo in the dictionary, you'd find Kyle's picture. Badass car, gorgeous girlfriend, money, looks… It almost wasn't fair. Although, even Tristan had to admit Kyle had been more chill, *happier* the last six weeks or so since he got together with Faith. Maybe that's what Tristan needed—a girl.

He snorted. Eight months out of a two-year relationship

had him rusty. The idea of trying to hook up with a girl sounded like more effort than he could spare right now.

"Dude, it's going to be fine." This from Dylan, the dream-crusher. "I'm just awesome today, is all."

"Don't be a jackass and kick him while he's stewing," Kyle said, giving them both a dose of his stern team-captain stare. "Go home, get some rest. It's going to be a long haul if we want to make it all the way to state."

Right. "Will do, boss."

Dylan followed Tristan to the locker room. "Seriously, stop pouting."

"If I hadn't known you since second grade…" Tristan made a fist. They both knew he was bluffing. Besides, he was being a baby about it. His swing *always* came back. "I'll be fine. Want to grab some dinner?"

Dylan laughed. "Is your Mom cooking tonight?"

"Yeah." Tristan shuddered. "I told her I might have study group. At Snap's."

"Okay, I'll be your cover. Seriously, your mother operates on people's hearts… You'd think she'd learn to cook."

Tristan shrugged his equipment bag onto his shoulder. "You'd think. Dad can grill things sort of okay, but it's 'casserole night,' so I'm having a burger."

"You buying?"

"Sure. As long as you don't rag me from the mound anymore."

"Dinner's on me, then!" Dylan grinned at him. "Just kidding. I'll stop busting on you."

"Uh-huh, and the first fastball I send over the fence will end that."

"Probably." Dylan looked way too cheerful about it. "Take me to dinner, sweetheart."

"You better put out later," Tristan grumbled.

Snap's was the best sports bar and restaurant this side of Dallas…and Tristan had his own booth.

"Back again?" His favorite server, Kathy, shook her head. She looked like somebody's frizzy-haired favorite aunt, right down to the shrewd gaze and mischievous smile. Like she'd sneak you into an R-rated movie and not tell your parents. "Seriously, take a load off your folks and learn to cook. Maybe you'll be good at it."

"Then I wouldn't see *you* three times a week." Tristan flashed her a smile.

She rolled her eyes. "Aren't you sweet."

After she took their order and left, Dylan put both hands flat on the table and announced, "So, there's this girl."

Tristan leaned back in his seat. "Seriously? After last year, I thought Dylan 'Ice Man' Dennings said girls were off the table until he made the minors. This must be some girl. Who is she?"

"Girl in my AP history class. Not super tall, but not short either. Fills out a T-shirt, if you know what I'm saying."

"No, Dylan, I have no idea." Tristan kicked him under the table. "Continue, Captain Obvious."

"Ow, Jesus. Anyhow, she has curly-ish hair and these big green eyes. Never seen anything like them. I dropped a pile of homework, and she helped me pick it up. Those eyes nearly knocked me over."

If it wasn't a girl's eyes, it was her hair, or her legs, or her smile. Or her ass. Dylan had a deep admiration for the female form. Then again, what seventeen-year-old guy didn't? Tristan grunted. Still, Dylan didn't usually do more than notice and move on. "Okay, Romeo, why don't you ask her out?"

"I need to keep my focus. Maybe once we win state." Dylan puffed his chest out. "That should make her give me a look, don't you think?"

Tristan gave him an amused smile. *He really has no clue.* None of the girls he'd been friends with or gone out with had given a crap about baseball. But Tristan wouldn't burst his friend's bubble. "It might."

While Dylan alternated between attacking his burger like his life depended on it and giving an enthusiastic play-by-play about how he would eventually ask History Girl out, Tristan picked at his dinner. The fries were perfect—thick cut, just the right amount of crispiness—but he couldn't shovel them down like Dylan. The tourney started tomorrow. *Tomorrow.* No matter what kind of brave face he put on, Tristan had a growing sense of alarm, and it was messing with his appetite. No surprise there. Because he was hiding something from the team: today wasn't the first time his swing had deserted him. No, it had been slowly slipping for the last two weeks.

He had to figure out a way to shake off his slump before he ruined the playoffs. Otherwise, his future as team captain would pass him by...and end up going to his best friend.

Chapter Three

ALYSSA

"That you, honey?" Mom called from the kitchen. The smell of homemade spaghetti sauce wafted through the house, and Alyssa's stomach growled right on cue.

"Yeah." She dumped her bag on the floor by the door and followed the smell of dinner.

Mom was busy stirring the sauce, the rising steam making her curly hair frizz at the edges. Alyssa had the same problem on humid days…and they lived in Texas. When *wasn't* there a humid day?

She leaned over the stove anyway, taking a good whiff of the sauce. She wouldn't eat much of the spaghetti, but she'd damn well enjoy every bite she took. "Where's Dad?"

"Closing up a little late. Said he had some paperwork to look over." Mom gave her a tired smile. Most of her smiles were tired. She was a nurse practitioner at a busy hospital and worked twelve-hour shifts.

"You two need a vacation, I think." Alyssa put an arm

around her Mom's shoulders. "Me, too, but if I get into the conservatory, I'll count that as mine. Maybe while I'm there, you two can run down to Galveston for a few days."

"Hmm, we'll see." Mom kissed her cheek. "Such a good girl, worrying about her parents."

Was it weird that she *was* worried about them? Their marriage was fine, as far as Alyssa could tell. They kissed each other in front of her and joked around, but there'd been a strain around the house for the last month or two, and Mom hadn't gotten the new car she and Dad had talked about last year. They weren't flat broke, but something was definitely not going right. Alyssa just wished they'd talk to her about it instead of keeping her in the dark to protect her. She was seventeen, for God's sake. She could take it, whatever *it* was.

A sharp bark warned her of impending doom. Claws skittered on the tile, then their beagle, Buddy, was butting his head against her knees, demanding her attention. *All* her attention.

"Did the silliest dog in all of Suttonville miss me?" She looked at the floor. Muddy footprints led from the dog door to where she stood. Good thing she'd worn shorts today—there were muddy paw prints on her shins, too. "Doofus."

Buddy barked and ran in a joyful circle. She hauled him out to the patio to wash his paws, just as her mom cried, "Buddy!"

"I got it!"

Buddy didn't love having his paws washed, but she scrubbed at them with an old towel no matter how he felt about it. She was almost done when her father's voice carried through the screen door.

"They finalized the report. It's not good."

Buddy wiggled in her arms, but she shushed him and leaned closer to listen.

"How long do we have?"

"Thirty days."

"Thirty days?" Her mom sounded shocked. "How much?"

"Ten grand, give or take a few hundred."

"Grant…we've already refinanced the house. Where are we going to get the money?"

Alyssa hugged Buddy tight. She was right—something was wrong. Her dad grunted in frustration. "I don't know. I'll…think of something, Rachel. I always do."

Buddy let out a bark and tore from her arms, chasing after some birds that had landed in the backyard.

"Uh-oh," Mom muttered, then louder, "Alyssa, it's time to come in now."

"Traitor," she muttered in Buddy's direction. He rolled onto his back and wiggled in the grass in answer.

Alyssa stood and stepped into the kitchen. Her dad gave her a semi-guilty look before smiling. "Get your homework done?"

"Yeah." She pulled out a chair and sat across from him, nailing him with a serious stare. "What's this about ten grand?"

Her parents exchanged a glance, and for a minute, Alyssa thought they were going to blow her off. Finally, her dad sighed. "It's Swing Away. Top Sports has put a squeeze on the business. Then we got inspected."

"By who?"

"The city. It happens." Her dad toyed with the salt shaker. "Anyway, they found some things they need us to fix…or shut down."

Alyssa's chest grew hot. "Who cares if two of our pitching machines are broken—"

"And some of our nets have too many holes. Safety hazard. And our parking lot isn't up to the new ADA codes. And there's a leak in the roof. I can't say it any other way, Chickadee. Swing Away is falling apart, and we won't be able to open our doors if we don't get it fixed."

Mom set the spaghetti on the table and handed pasta bowls around. "That takes money. But don't worry. We'll... come up with something"

Looking at their faces, though, Alyssa knew they really couldn't. They were out of options. She wasn't, though. She had two thousand saved up. "There's my dance camp money. Maybe we use that, and I can get a new part-time job."

"No." Dad's tone was forceful. "You worked two years for that dance camp money, and we aren't spending it."

"But we don't even know if I'll pass the audition."

Mom put an arm around her shoulders. "You will. So you'll need the money. Maybe I can work some overtime."

Her parents gave her false smiles, but there was no way Mom could work that much overtime in thirty days. And Alyssa's two grand wouldn't be enough, either.

If they couldn't find the money, their family's batting cages would close. For good.

Alyssa pushed her spaghetti away. "I'm not hungry. I'm going to bed."

Her parents didn't stop her, but a clacking of claws on the tile and the thump of paws down the hallway to her room let her know she wasn't going alone. Buddy jumped onto her bed, wagging his tail. She settled down next to him and pressed her forehead against his side.

Her tears wet his fur, but Buddy stayed in the circle of her arms. "What are we going to do, dog?"

Buddy let out a short bark.

"You don't happen to have ten grand buried in a hole in the yard do you?"

He licked her cheek. A no, then.

She sat up, petting him. She couldn't give up that easily. She'd grown up there—she wasn't letting it go without a fight. She had to find a way to save the business.

The real problem was figuring out how.

Chapter Four

TRISTAN

"All right! Let's give this all we've got," Coach said. "Smart plays, men. No stupid mistakes. Errors cost games. Full attention, every second. We can beat Coppell, no problem. You just have to want it more."

Everyone nodded. Then Kyle yelled, "Let's go, Sentinels!"

They yelled it back, and the starters jogged up the dugout steps to wait for the anthem to be played. Dylan had taken a spot next Tristan. "Dude, what's up with the shaky hands?"

"What?" Tristan looked at his glove—it was trembling. Damn it. "Nothing. Just excited. That's all."

"Don't let the monster get into your head." Dylan pulled his hat off and put it over his heart. "That's how the spiral starts."

But what if it's already started? Tristan clenched his hands during the anthem, trying to fight off the shakes. They didn't usually have a big crowd at the games, but tonight the stands were packed. They were the higher seed, so they got to play at home. Somehow, that felt worse.

"Play ball!" the umpire yelled, and they ran to their positions. At least they got to field first. His catching and throwing were still just fine.

Mark, their third-spot pitcher, was on point, striking out the first batter and only allowing the second a short pop that the second baseman easily fielded. The third batter, though, cracked one hard. Tristan and Kyle turned to run for it, but there was nothing to do—the ball sailed over the fence.

Mark grimaced as the Coppell player ran the bases. The first baseman yelled some encouragement his way as the catcher came out to talk him down. One run wasn't the end of the world, but it did mean they needed a hit. Tristan batted fourth—clean up—with Kyle fifth. One of them would need to be a hero and hope the first three guys didn't get out on an easy pitch.

Mark settled down and struck out the next batter, and they cleared the field.

"Good job. Way to hold it together." Coach nodded as Mark passed by. "All right, we're up. We need a score. Answer them."

Dylan, who'd been pacing and watching Mark like he always did when someone else pitched, plopped down next to Tristan. His hair, bleached blond from the sun, stuck out from under his cap. When he didn't make a move to fix it— unusual, because Dylan was a neat freak—Tristan knew they were both worried about this game.

"You better hit something," Dylan said. "Seriously. At least get on base for Kyle."

"That's assuming we don't go three and out."

Just as he said it, *ting!* Their leadoff man hit a long single. Dylan punched his shoulder. "Say that again."

"All right, all right." Tristan pulled his bat out of his bag and started doing small stretches, ignoring the little fizz of nerves in his stomach. *Shake it off. You've got this.*

The next batter failed to get on base but gave their leadoff guy a sacrifice fly to move him to second. The team cheered them on, but Tristan couldn't seem to open his mouth. Mainly because he was afraid he'd puke.

God, he hated this. Why did he have to be so damn afraid of something he loved? Didn't matter—it was his turn in the on-deck circle.

"Scoring position," Dylan hissed as he went by.

"I know, dumbass." He went up the stairs to stretch and await his turn.

The third batter struck out swinging, and Tristan heard the collective groans of his teammates. Taking a shaky breath, he went to the plate.

Even as he raised the bat, he could tell something was off, wrong. The first pitch was a fastball, straight down the middle. He'd read somewhere that a good fastball was ninety miles an hour, but a batter could only swing at seventy miles an hour. That gave the batter something like 0.2 seconds to decide whether or not to swing.

This pitch had caught him napping.

Cursing himself, he stepped out of the batter's box and swung a few times. It was nothing. He was overthinking it.

And apparently still was when a pitch that was *way* too high came by…and he whiffed it.

"Strike," the umpire called.

He was 0 and 2. Grinding his teeth, Tristan stepped back into the box. He'd get it. *This time.* The pitcher wound up and threw. Changeup. Tristan gauged the distance and swung.

"Strike! You're out."

The outfield was coming in, and his teammates were coming out. Kyle sent him a reassuring nod as he jogged by. The rest of the team stared at him. Astonished? Pissed? He'd blown a good scoring opportunity. He'd let them down.

Cursing aloud now, he retrieved his glove and jogged out to center field. He had to get it together.

"Look, it's not the end of the world," Kyle said, settling onto the locker room bench to pull off his cleats. "We won, and that's what matters. You had that brilliant catch in the seventh to save us from two runs… So what if you had a little trouble at the plate?"

"A little trouble? First, Mark wrenches his elbow in the seventh and lets one last run through." Tristan slammed his locker shut. A sophomore looked over the top of the locker bank, glaring. He glared back. "Then I went O-fer. The last time I didn't get at least one hit in a game? Fourteen months ago. I always get at least a single."

"It's not a slump. Quit building it up." Kyle reached into his locker for his phone. He grinned and started texting.

Tristan sighed and started packing up his bag. Not only had Kyle had two crucial hits, now he was basking in the glory with his girl.

Stop being a bitter asshole, asshole. He needed to figure this out. They'd play again next week, and twice more if they kept winning.

What he needed was a place to practice, away from everyone else. The team *owned* Top Sports on the weekends. All the guys went there for extra batting practice, which meant he needed to go somewhere else so he could focus.

Wait, what about that old place on the edge of town… Swing something or other? As long as it wasn't filled with Little Leaguers, that might be the perfect spot.

Tristan forced himself to take a few deep breaths. He had a plan. Things had to go up from here.

Chapter Five

Saturday morning, Alyssa awoke curled up around Buddy. Her pillow was damp, and she glared at it. "Cried yourself to sleep, huh? Loser."

After scratching Buddy behind the ears, she marched to the shower. It was after eight, and Dad usually wanted her at work by now. If she was going to take off early to work with Lauren and Faith on her audition, she needed to hurry. While she washed her hair, begging it to suddenly become sleek and straight, she tried to hold on to some hope that they'd save Swing Away.

Somehow.

When she was ready, she bounded to the kitchen, grabbing an apple on the way out. Mom was still asleep. She needed the rest, so Alyssa put the Honda in neutral and let it roll down the hill before starting it, just to make sure the grumbly engine didn't wake her. The morning was overcast and humid. They'd have a storm for sure this afternoon. Easy to predict that in mid-May in north Texas. Still, the air had a charge to it that spoke of seventy-mile-per-hour wind gusts and hail the size of oranges.

Swing Away's "open" sign was glowing in the window, and a few cars were in the lot. One was a minivan, which made her groan. Minivans brought terror to batting cages. A few looked like they belonged to baseball and softball moms—Suburbans with those decals that looked like a baseball had broken the back windshield.

And one newish Mustang.

Okay, *that* she didn't see every day.

Alyssa picked up some loose trash on the way inside. Anything to make the place look like somewhere to stop and spend some money.

Dad was at the check-in counter, pouring over a stack of receipts. He looked up when the bell above the door dinged. "Ah, you made it."

"Sorry." She paused, listening to the sounds of young elementary school kids arguing and a tired mother's voice trying to drown them out. "My punishment can be to go untangle whatever that mess is."

Dad saluted her with his coffee mug—thank God he hadn't sold the coffee maker for extra cash. She might've rioted. Instead, she dropped her backpack off in the little office and strode to the cage where the hellions were currently arguing over a bat.

A *bat*. They had *thirty-seven* aluminum bats lying around.

"It's mine!" a kid who appeared to be eight shouted.

A boy, six maybe, wailed, "No! It's mine!"

The mom covered her face with her hand. "Boys, stop, or we'll go."

Alyssa didn't believe that for one minute. "Is there a problem?"

"He took my bat!" the older kid said.

"Did not!"

"Did too!"

"Did not!"

"Stop. Now." Alyssa used her ultra-calm, you-better-listen-or-else voice. "What's so special about that one?"

"It's red!" the younger boy said.

"Okay, if you can stand still for sixty seconds without arguing, I might be able to fix this." She went to the bat rack, not waiting for an answer, because, there in plain view, was an identical bat. "Here."

The older boy snatched it out of her hands. "This one's mine!"

"Yeah, but mine's better." The younger kid stuck his tongue out.

"Whatever. Play ball." Alyssa spun on her heel and went back to the front counter. "Dad, please tell me you don't want grandkids."

He snorted. "Can you do a sweep of the cages, make sure everything is working?"

"Sure." She grabbed the small tool bag they kept under the counter, just in case, and started her rounds. Cages two and three held kids from a Little League team. The four of them were practicing under the watchful eye of their coach. The next one was filled with some middle schoolers there for fun, it seemed. Six had that family with the bickering kids. They seemed to be fine, except for the fact that *now* they were fighting over whose turn it was. Alyssa kept on walking.

Cages seven was empty. Cage eight, though. She frowned. Why had this guy come all the way back here? A real equipment bag—a *Suttonville High* baseball bag—lay open on the bench inside the cage. The boy at the plate looked familiar, maybe a junior like her? His light-brown hair was cut to military precision, and the rest of him looked as ripped as a soldier, too.

Damn.

He held the bat in an iron grip, his forearms and biceps flexed, and Alyssa leaned against the wall to watch. How could she not? It wasn't every day a hot guy her age dropped by Swing Away.

The pitching machine whirred, then spat out a ball: changeup, slightly low.

The boy swung, putting plenty of power behind it. If he'd taken a better look, he would've come down an inch. As it was, he tipped the ball with the top of the bat, and it fouled off.

"Goddamn it!" He shook his head and squared up again. The machine wound up, pitched—medium fastball, down the middle, *easy*—and the guy swung for the fences.

Whiff.

What the hell? Suttonville's team was really good, and based on last year's varsity patch on his bag, he'd been a starter at least a year already. Alyssa frowned and took a step closer. The guy was muttering at his bat again and didn't see her.

He readied himself, the machine whirred—curveball, perfect. He tipped it again. Cursing loudly, he tossed his bat into his bag and dropped to the bench with his face in his hands.

The mom a few cages down called, "Could you watch the language, please?" She had her hands over the little one's ears. The eight-year-old grinned like he was soaking up every word.

Alyssa waved at her. "I've got it."

She'd said it mostly to get the mom off this guy's back—because he looked seriously put out—but his head whipped around toward her. Oops… She was supposed to be spying. The guy's eyes narrowed. "What are you doing?"

"Coming down here to ask you to watch the language." There, that sounded like a reasonable excuse, right? On the other hand, she could drown in those chocolate-brown eyes. Maybe letting him stare at her with his mouth open wasn't a bad thing after all.

"Why? You own the place?" The words came out bitter, but she could tell it wasn't aimed at her.

"Actually, my dad does. I work here after school and on the weekends." She nodded to the pitching machine. "Is it off-kilter?"

Now, the machine looked fine to her, but if a guy like this kept missing, maybe that was the reason. *Sure…that's why he's here and not at Top Sports showing off for all the giggly girls.*

He pointed at her tool kit. "Could you look at it?"

"Yep." She opened the door and slid past him. There was a little gate at the bottom to keep people from tampering with the machines, so she unlocked it, holding up the keys to show him she really did work here. "Hmm, looks fine."

"It is me, then." The guy clunked his head against the chain-link wall behind the bench. "This is *not* the time for a slump."

Alyssa locked the gate and went back to the batter's box, looking the guy over again. For professional reasons, of course. Yeah, right. She had a rule about dating ballplayers—and customers—but this one might make her reconsider. "Show me."

"What?" His brow wrinkled, and he looked at her in confusion. "Show you what?"

"Hit a few."

He shook his head, giving her a wry smile. "I think I've hit enough. Besides…I mean, I have a batting coach."

"Uh-huh, and have you told him your timing is off and you're so stressed out you're pulling the bat when you swing?"

His jaw dropped. "How do you know?"

Alyssa lifted her chin in defiance. "I watched."

He still looked skeptical, so she grabbed the bat out of his bag, ignoring his protests, and started the machine.

Whirr, click: fastball, medium. Almost too easy.

Ting! The ball hit the back wall, just like it had for the Little Leaguers last night. Winking at the boy, she squared up for the next pitch—curveball, low—and let it go by.

"Sometimes they throw out balls rather than strikes. They shouldn't, but if they've been on a while, a few will be duds," she said, before turning back to watch the machine.

Whirr, click: changeup, strike zone. She paused, then swung, slower than the first time.

Ting!

That should do it. Giving the boy a quick, coy smile, she turned off the machine and handed his bat to him. "Timing and stress. Bad combo, my friend. By the way, you look familiar. I go to Suttonville, too. I'm a junior."

He nodded, looking tired. He probably was—they played last night and probably got home late. He had to be operating on fumes. She sighed. Male ego at its finest.

"I'm Alyssa. And you need to lay off for a while. You're only going to make it worse if you don't rest your body."

He nodded again, and she could see the dark circles under his eyes. "I'm Tristan. And...thanks."

She sat down next to him. "I imagine you're here because it's out of the way, and you don't want the team around while you work this stuff out, right?"

Tristan stood abruptly. "Look, you've been nice about all this, but I think I should go."

He started shoving his gear back into his bag, and Alyssa watched him. Ego was a pain in the ass, especially with a cute boy. Maybe her rule not to date customers or ballplayers could stand. "Suit yourself. If you decide you'd like some coaching outside the circle of trust, I'm here from four to six most afternoons, when I don't have group projects. And all day Saturdays and two to four on Sunday afternoons. I don't even charge for coaching. All you have to do is buy a few rounds."

"Yeah…thanks." Tristan wouldn't even look at her. "Nice meeting you."

She watched his back as he hurried out of the building. "Ballplayers."

Shrugging, she got up to help the mom pry her screaming kids apart. Again.

Chapter Six

TRISTAN

After all that, he *still* ran into someone from school. Tristan recognized the girl, too—she was a dancer friend of Kyle's girlfriend. Alyssa, so that was her name…and now she knew his secret. What if she told Faith, and it got back to Kyle? The team knew something was off, but it wouldn't be long before they knew how bad it was.

Alyssa said it was stress. No kidding. He didn't think she could help him, despite her being able to crush a ball. How did a dancer know how to do that, though? Working at a batting cage, it must've rubbed off.

Tristan slumped in the driver's seat of his Mustang and ran a hand over his face. He had to admit one thing—the girl wasn't hard on the eyes. Curvy, with thick, curly, dark-brown hair a guy could get lost in… Any other day, he might've turned on the charm, but today he was too wound up to do anything. Maybe she was right about getting more rest.

The winding road up to Lakeside usually calmed him

down as he drove home. Today, the lake sparkled between the leaves, calling, "Get in the boat, Tristan. Come play…"

One more month—if they were lucky—then he could hang out on the lake all he wanted.

He pulled into the driveway and parked by the side of the house. No point in putting the car in the garage or carrying his bag inside—he'd have to leave in two hours anyway. He could only hope that by the time practice was over, he'd be in a better place, with his swing—and his swagger—back.

"I'm home!" he yelled on his way to the stairs. From the sound of things, Dad was watching a documentary on the space program.

"Just in time." Dad waved at him over the leather sofa's back. "They're talking about the Apollo missions."

The last thing he felt like doing was watching educational TV. "Sorry. Homework."

Dad turned around to peer at him. "Homework over television? Are you feeling okay?"

"Fine, just busy." Tristan jogged up the stairs before Mom came out to check his temperature. She'd be back from rounds by now and ready to fret over her baby's health. His older brother never had to put up with it, but he was also still at college until finals were over.

Tristan's room had a lake view, and he went straight to the window to look out. Boats dragged skiers in the distance, and ducks floated on his end of the lake. His dad had a saying about ducks: good leaders are like ducks—they're calm and collected on the surface, but paddle like hell underneath. Maybe that was his problem. He needed to smooth his nerves, stop letting it bother him, and let his instincts take over. He didn't know when he had *stopped* doing that, but he needed to get there again.

He sprawled on his bed, toying with his phone. His thoughts drifted to Alyssa. Maybe he needed to be more like her. She struck him as coolly confident and certain in her own talent.

But that wasn't why he was thinking about her, was it? She was pretty, but there was something else. She was so *normal*, not hyper or giggly like some of the other girls he knew. Or had dated. She carried a tool bag, and there was something sexy about that. And her T-shirt couldn't hide all those curves. He didn't like rail-thin girls. She was just the right amount of athletic and feminine to get his attention.

But Dylan has a point—she needs to be off-limits until the season's over, stupid.

Sighing, he flopped onto his stomach and took a nap.

"Murrell, you're up." Coach pointed at him. "Morris needs the practice."

Out on the mound, Jackson Morris grimaced. They had three starting pitchers, and after one got hurt, he'd rotated up to varsity. Dylan was having a rest day, thank God. Even with his problems, Tristan could hit off a green sophomore.

He stepped into the batter's box. His nap had unwound some of the tension in his shoulders. Maybe there was something to Alyssa's advice after all.

Jackson threw a fastball, straight down the middle. His speed was slower than Dylan's, and Tristan actually got a piece of it, probably a long single. Better, but that had been a grapefruit, swing-for-the-fence kind of pitch.

Jackson wound up and pitched again. To Tristan's surprise, the kid had a wicked curveball. He swung at it and caught nothing but air.

Jackson grinned. Tristan glared at him. The next pitch was another fastball, low and outside. Tristan's turn to grin. He paid for it. Jackson threw a changeup, and Tristan swung and missed again.

And again.

Finally, Coach put him out of his misery. "Murrell, you're done. Sawyer, go on up there."

Tristan had barely sat down in the dugout before *Ting!* The guys around him jumped up and watched. Dylan whistled. "I hope no one was parked across the street."

Tristan slumped against the bench as Kyle nailed three more balls in succession.

After practice, Jackson came up to him with a shrewd glance. "Your hitting game is off."

"No shit," Tristan muttered. "Here to trash-talk?"

"Nope. You know what you need?" Jackson asked. "A slumpbuster."

Tristan frowned, suspicious. Jackson could be a complete punk sometimes. "What's that?"

"Find yourself a DUFF, get laid." Jackson grinned. "Supposedly works. It's gotta be a real plain girl, though. Not someone you'd usually hook up with. Otherwise it doesn't count."

Tristan's fists curled. "That's awful, asshat."

Jackson shrugged. "Not as awful as your two-week batting average. We're counting on you. I don't think most of the other guys notice, but Coach does. You need to get it together."

He strolled off, whistling.

Dylan came up behind Tristan. "I'll go hard on him during pitching practice Tuesday. He deserves to have his head deflated a little."

"Yeah. I think he does."

"Look, it's not a slump. It's…a correction." Dylan swatted him on the arm with his glove. "Want to hit Snap's? I'll even buy this time."

"Sure. What about Sawyer?"

"Plans with Faith." Dylan snorted. "Which is going to be

the answer to that question for a while, I think."

"Probably." Tristan paused. "So, there's this girl."

Dylan's face lit up. "Really? *Really?* I thought after you and Raina broke up you'd hibernate for a while."

"This girl is pretty hard to ignore. Cute, good personality." From what he'd seen anyway. Sassy was the word that came to mind, and he liked sassy. "I wonder if I should leave it alone until after playoffs, though. Like you said, we need to focus."

"You know what? I decided not to wait on that girl I like from history. No time like the present, man. Seize the day, or some shit like that." Dylan nodded firmly. "If I can do it, so can you. So, our mission is to talk to these girls, and see what happens."

"Wait." Tristan laughed. "You haven't even *talked* to her yet? This girl with the amazing green eyes? That girl? From your chatter the other night, I figured you'd been hitting her up already."

"I loaned her a pencil once." Dylan hung his head in shame. "But no."

"Okay, I agree to the mission." Tristan pointed a finger at Dylan. "Which means by practice on Monday, I want a report that you spoke to her."

"Deal."

They left the field, and Tristan felt better than he had for two weeks. He'd go to Swing Away tomorrow, talk to Alyssa. And maybe, just maybe, ask her to diagnose his swing.

Or out for coffee. It was a toss-up.

Chapter Seven

Alyssa put the last of the chips bags into the display at the snack bar, then went to find her dad. "Faith is practicing with Lauren and me at four. Madame Schuler let her open the studio up just for us."

Dad checked his watch and glanced at the cages. Only one was in use. On a Saturday during baseball season, they should've been running a wait. "Looks like I can handle it."

"Dad…" She paused. What could she say to make anything better? "Take my dance company money. Please."

"No." He smiled at her. "You love to dance. I'm not taking that away from you. What I *am* going to do is drive to the bank on Monday morning and apply for a small business loan. Ten thousand isn't too much to fuss over. Mom and I wanted to avoid the debt, but if it'll save the business, we'll do it."

Alyssa clenched her jaw shut against the torrent of words she wanted to say. Either Dad would be approved for the loan, or he wouldn't. Arguing about her dance money wouldn't change that. She nodded. "Sounds good. I'll be home around six thirty."

"Okay. Have a good rehearsal." He started pulling receipts from the register. That was something they did at close, not in the middle of the afternoon. Did he not expect any more customers today?

She forced a smile. "I will."

Once she cleared the front door, she let the smile fall. Helplessness wasn't an emotion she enjoyed, so she worked hard to avoid it. Today, she couldn't.

She kicked a rock on the gravel drive, sending it skidding into the field next to the building. She needed to think about something else, otherwise her muscles would be tight, and that would ruin her rehearsal.

Sending her brain to a happy place was easy. Finding Tristan standing there, in her imagination, was different. She hadn't really expected that. They had some things in common—both juniors, both ballplayers, both seething with frustration over something that was pretty difficult to control. And he was definitely cute. Great shoulders, flat stomach, brown eyes. A girl magnet for sure.

So, what did she do? She'd given him *batting advice*. Almost like she was saying, "Hey hot boy, you suck at baseball."

She probably wouldn't see him ever again. Not unless they ran into each other at school. She hardly knew him anyway. That swooping feeling… That wasn't disappointment. That was…heartburn or something. She did eat popcorn for lunch.

Alyssa drove into town, arriving at Madame Schuler's studio a few minutes early. Faith's little yellow Bug was already there, next to a black Charger, but Lauren's Mazda was nowhere to be found. She'd probably be ten minutes late, like usual, so Alyssa went inside to do some stretches before her best friend arrived. Having Faith help them was too precious to waste. She'd be graduating soon, leaving Madame Schuler without her current prima, and Alyssa without a dance coach. Lauren could be late if she wanted, but Alyssa wanted every minute of Faith's instruction that she could get.

Music poured out of the bigger studio toward the back of the building, beckoning her inside. Tchaikovsky? She rounded the corner and stopped outside the observation window, her jaw on the floor.

Faith was dancing…and she wasn't alone.

"A little higher?" she asked.

Kyle, who was holding her at shoulder level, laughed. "You're kidding, right? I don't think either of us can handle a full extension."

She dipped her face toward his. "I know all kinds of ways to encourage you."

"You do, huh? Okay, then." Kyle's biceps flexed, and up Faith went.

Alyssa's cheeks flamed. Despite the banter, the scene was a little more intimate than she expected. Kyle wasn't wearing a shirt for one thing…and both of them were barefoot. Practicing contemporary dance, most likely, but *still*. Kyle was holding Faith up by her thigh and her waist, his arms and chest straining. They were like a freaking Michelangelo statue. He rotated slowly, then twisted Faith to help her slide around his body to the floor.

"Coach saw me doing this, he'd lose his shit. Risk of injury."

"Yeah, well." Faith patted him on the chest. "Call it strength training."

The door to the lobby slammed shut, and Alyssa jumped into the hallway, praying Faith and Kyle didn't see her. She should've known who the Charger belonged to. Why had she come in early? Why?

Lauren stopped just inches away. "What are you doing?"

"Trying not to be a third wheel," Alyssa whispered. "Faith's in there with Kyle."

Lauren glanced around her, and her eyebrows shot up. "Damn, Sawyer. Been working out, I see."

There was a self-conscious laugh, and a moment later, Kyle breezed by them, wearing a shirt and carrying his shoes. "She's all yours."

"You didn't have to quit on our account." Lauren winked at him.

Kyle rolled his eyes. "Faith, I'll see you at seven."

"Bye!" Faith called, as Alyssa and Lauren shuffled inside. "Sorry about that. I was offered a second audition at Elon, and they wanted to see some contemporary work, with a partner."

"Kyle's going to be in the audition?" Lauren jabbed a thumb toward the front door. "Kyle *Sawyer*?"

Faith laughed. "Full of surprises, isn't he? Why don't you two warm up, and we'll start with Vivaldi?"

Alyssa sat down to tie on her pointe shoes. "I knew she was going to say that."

"It's the hardest part." Lauren sounded cheerful about it. "That's where we need the work."

Sighing, Alyssa stood and went to the barre to stretch. This part felt good. Some of her stress released along with her muscles, and she leaned in, curving her body over her extended right leg. Much better.

Spring from Vivaldi's *The Four Seasons* began over the speakers. The tempo was quick, and the music was light…and technically difficult to dance to. Which was the point.

Alyssa lined up next to Lauren as the audition section began. In the mirror, Lauren stood with perfect posture, her arms graceful above her head. Alyssa knew she was no slouch, but Lauren was the company's second, behind Faith.

Most of the dance went fine, even though Alyssa couldn't

turn off the part of her brain that worried about Swing Away, until they reached the bourée section. Normally, en pointe work was Alyssa's best, given her strong legs and ankles, but today, she stumbled and came down.

The music stopped, and Faith turned to her, frowning. "What happened?"

"Not sure." Okay, that was a lie. Her mind wasn't sticking with the program. "Can we rerun that last section?"

Faith nodded, and the piece started again. Alyssa finished the dance without issue but wasn't satisfied. From the way Faith was chewing her lip, she wasn't either.

"Hmm. So, Lauren, you rushed ahead of the music a few times. *Listen.* Don't count, move with the music." Faith closed her eyes and swayed back and forth. "Be a part of it. The moves should be second nature to the spirit of the dance."

Lauren nodded, giving Alyssa a quick smile. "She caught me."

Faith shrugged. "That's what you're…not paying me for. Alyssa, do you feel like you understand the flow of the routine, or was it a mental issue? Because you looked a hundred miles away."

That stung, but she was impressed Faith could see that much. She'd make a great teacher somewhere, someday. "I have some stuff on my mind."

"This will sound bad, but leave your brain at the door." Faith waggled her eyebrows. "Lead with your heart and your body. Whatever has you stressed, see if you can't let it go for a little while. Let dancing be your sanctuary."

That was the thing—dance *was* her sanctuary. Sometimes, though, problems grew big enough to invade everything. "Sure thing, boss."

Faith patted Alyssa's arm. "Good. Okay, so let's break this thing down, section by section."

"Did you see those pecs?" Lauren nudged Alyssa with her hip. "Kyle looks like a walking, breathing underwear model."

Alyssa grunted. "I saw him in the musical. If you would've tried out, you could've ogled him every night for a few weeks."

"Not with his shirt off." Lauren let out a theatrical sigh. "Where's *my* hot baseball player?"

"There are eighteen of them at every varsity game. Go shopping."

Lauren's cheeks turned pink. "Oh, I've already picked one out. Not sure he knows I exist, though."

"Who is it?"

Her cheeks went from pink to fuchsia. "You know what, it's stupid. I, um, I don't actually know his name. I've been too embarrassed to ask."

Alyssa stopped walking. "*You?* But you talk to everyone. Sometimes without filters."

"I know! Isn't that weird?" She leaned against her Mazda. "Think Faith could introduce me?"

"Sure." Alyssa paused, thinking about Tristan. "But maybe you ought to try talking to him first. Stop him in the hall and ask him if he's on the team, and wish him luck in the playoffs. Athletes like the attention."

"Would you come with me?"

Alyssa shook her head, laughing. "We aren't in seventh grade, Laur. I'll walk that way with you, but I'm stopping twenty paces away and letting you handle this."

She nodded, looking nervous. Very un-Lauren-like. Even with her blond hair up in a perfect ballerina bun, she looked much younger than seventeen.

She must have it bad. "You can do this." She gave Lauren a hug. "I need to run. Mom's working, and I should probably cook something for dinner so Dad and I don't end up microwaving a pizza."

"Why don't you come out with me? We can go to Dolly's for a burger…" She paused, looking uncomfortable. "Or, um, Ensalata for salads."

The back of Alyssa's neck grew warm. "No, it's fine. I'll see you Monday."

Lauren nodded, and they drove out of the studio going in opposite directions. Alyssa sighed. It wasn't just the calories, it was the money that kept her from going out, but she didn't want to explain that to Lauren, because then she'd offer to buy.

There'd been enough uncomfortable moments today. Alyssa didn't need to add one more.

Chapter Eight

TRISTAN

Sunday mornings were lazy around Tristan's house. Mom did rounds really early so she could hang out on the couch with Dad and watch old movies. And, even better, she always bought bagels for breakfast. The one and only time she'd tried to make eggs and pancakes, they'd needed a fire extinguisher.

Hey, at least she tried.

Tristan helped himself to a bagel and cream cheese and went out to the back porch. The mornings were warming up fast, but it wasn't hot yet. Out here, he could think. The wind rustled through the big oaks in their backyard, and birds sang to each other across the trees. None of them cared that his batting average was in danger of dropping below two fifty for the first time since freshman year.

Alyssa said she worked two to four today. Tristan leaned back in his chair, wondering if she'd really meant it when she'd offered to help. Probably so, and she had the skills to back it up. Maybe that would be a good opportunity to find out if she had a boyfriend. God, if she did…that would suck.

The back door creaked open, and Dad came outside. "It's nice out here."

"Yep."

His dad settled into the patio chair next to him. "You okay? You've been kind of quiet lately."

Tristan shrugged. His dad meant well, but they weren't all that alike. His father was wearing "dad jeans" with a plaid shirt and beat-up tennis shoes—the thick-soled, mostly white kind you mainly saw on grandpas at the mall. His glasses had slipped down his nose, too. He looked like a physics professor with nineteen patents…which he was. Between his genius dad, and a mom who operated on people's hearts and lungs every day, Tristan always wondered if he'd been adopted. Except he'd heard both of them tell their friends, "We're not quite sure how we had an athlete."

This was always said with a self-deprecating laugh, and Tristan always smiled like it was the funniest thing ever. His older brother was the brain. He was at MIT majoring in electrical engineering, and the parents were *so proud*. It's not like they didn't support Tristan, but it wasn't the same. Even though they came to Tristan's home games, he could tell it was for him, and not because they enjoyed the sport. When other guys were out playing catch with their dad, his was trying to read him passages from *A Brief History of Time*.

So when his dad asked, "Are you okay?" the answer had to be "yes."

He wouldn't understand a hitting slump. Or the fact that his heart still hurt a little from his breakup. Or that he might, possibly, have a crush on a girl whose dad owned a batting cage clubhouse. His dreams of going into the minors after college and working his way up to the major league wouldn't even compute.

Tristan changed the subject. "When is Keller coming home?"

"He said his last final is a week from Tuesday, so he'll be here in time to watch the last few games of the playoffs." Dad smiled. "He's sure you'll still be in it by then."

Someone had faith in his team—in *him*—which felt good. "It'll be nice having him around for a little while."

Dad laughed outright. "I never thought I'd live to see the day you were actually glad to see your brother."

Yeah, because his brother knew enough about baseball to be a good sounding board. "Weird, huh?"

"Yes, a little." His dad shoved his glasses up his nose. "Have your SAT scores come in yet? We need to get a jump on college applications."

They had, but he wasn't ready to share those yet. His brother had scored a fifteen-forty—and was still bitter about missing a few questions. Tristan's score was respectably average. Even a little above. But an eleven-twenty wasn't the same, and his parents would see it as a failure, even if they didn't say so…and even though it wasn't.

He reached for his bagel so he wouldn't have to look at his dad. "I'll probably get them next week."

"Hmm, running a bit late this year. Oh, well." He ruffled Tristan's hair. "What are your plans today?"

"Some batting practice, finishing up my homework. Nothing special."

"Sounds good." Dad gave him a long, sort of concerned look, then got up and went inside.

Tristan let out a long breath. He needed to get out of here. It was barely noon now, but Swing Away would be open. Maybe he should go now and be there, waiting, when Alyssa came in.

Nodding, he broke off pieces of his unfinished bagel and fed them to the birds.

The man at the counter looked up as soon as the little bell over the front door dinged. He had wavy brown hair, the same shade as Alyssa's, so this must be her dad. "Welcome. Didn't I see you yesterday?"

"Yes, sir. I'm trying to sneak in some batting practice between regular practices." He held up his Suttonville baseball team bag. "There's a big game next week."

Her dad brightened—Tristan really needed to learn Alyssa's last name so he could call the guy something. "You guys are doing great this year. I didn't get to last week's game, but we're going this week. I wish you luck. How about some rounds on the house?"

Tristan looked around. The place definitely needed some TLC, and it was empty. "I appreciate it, but I'm happy to pay."

He forked over a twenty, and Alyssa's dad sent Tristan to cage four, which was closer to the front. "Um, could I go to seven? I like it because it's off by itself."

"Sure thing." He led Tristan down to cage seven and turned everything on. "Enjoy."

Tristan did some stretches and took a few practice swings before turning on the machine. He let the first ball go through, then squared up. The machine made a clanking sound and a ball flew out. Tristan swung, getting a piece of it. It would've been a foul pop, but it felt good to connect. He caught the edge of the next one, too, but his luck started to wear off. Four balls later, he had yet to get a real hit off any of them.

Cursing under his breath, he switched to a wooden bat. They played with aluminum in the school league, but he liked the feel of a good wooden bat in his hands. The sound it made— *crack!*—was so much better than the *ting!* of a metal bat.

He went to the batter's box again and started the machine. He whiffed the first four, caught the edge of the fifth, and finally hit the sixth in something that resembled a base hit. Granted, it should've been a solid double, but at least he hit it.

"Back at it?"

Tristan paused the machine and turned. Alyssa stood outside the cage, wearing a pair of those short running shorts girls liked to wear and guys liked to see. Her legs were strong and lean. He had a hard time keeping his eyes off of them, but it was rude to stare so he forced his gaze to her face. She had her curly hair pulled back, but it fought to get loose. He wished he could steal her ponytail holder, see all that hair down and soft.

"You in there?" she asked, a smile tugging at the corners of her mouth. "I forgot to ask the other day. What's your last name?"

"Murrell. You?"

"Kaplan." She motioned at the gate. "Mind if I join you?"

His heart beat a little faster. He'd forgotten this—how a little attraction made everything seem bigger. "Come on in. You can watch me stink up the place."

Yep, that was exactly *the right thing to tell a girl you might be interested in.*

She laughed, though, and it wasn't mean. "You don't stink. You just have a kink in your swing. My offer still stands, if you'd like some free coaching."

He took a step closer to her, smiling when she didn't step away. "I would. I've swallowed my pride, dashed my ego, slowed my swagger. I need help, Kaplan."

"The first step is admitting you have a problem." She looked up at him, her eyes crinkled at the corners. "And your problem is fixable."

He was nodding, totally sucked in by her eyes. Her lashes were long and thick, framing the most amazing pair of green eyes he'd ever seen. Something about that sounded familiar, but he couldn't think straight, and didn't want to.

"I'm all yours."

Chapter Nine

Tristan was staring at her. Not in a bad way, but it made her feel exposed. It wasn't every day that a hot guy stared at her like he'd just come in from the desert and she was an oasis.

"Uh, okay." She turned to fiddle with the machine so he wouldn't see her flaming cheeks. "Close your eyes."

A soft laugh made her look up at him. He grinned at her, and the blush crept from her cheeks down her chest. "That's a promising start."

She stood and put a hand on her hip, giving him a "cut the crap" look. "I'm checking for inner ear and balance issues."

The grin slid off his face, and his eyebrows went up. "For real?"

"No, I want to take a picture of you with your eyes closed. Of *course* for real."

Shaking out his arms, he picked up a bat, then stepped into the batter's box. Once his eyes were closed, she walked around him, frowning. Okay, maybe she lingered a second too long checking out his ass. Tristan really was cute, but she was here to do a job.

She watched him for a full thirty seconds. He was completely still.

Okay, time for the real test. "Lift your right foot. Keep your eyes closed."

He looked skeptical but did as she asked. His balance was excellent.

"Okay, you can relax and open your eyes."

"Well, doc?" he asked. "What's my diagnosis?"

She frowned, worried about the hope in his voice. What if she couldn't help him? Or made it *worse*? "Don't know yet. You are really well balanced in your stance, so the problem must be in your swing itself."

"Or between my ears," he muttered.

That was probably more true than he thought. "When's the last time you had your eyes checked?"

"Two months ago. Twenty-twenty, like always."

She liked how he said that—not cocky or boasting…just honest. So many elite athletes were gods in their own minds. Tristan seemed more grounded. In fact, she was pretty sure he needed more confidence, not less. She gave him a sidelong look. His shoulders were slumped a little. Yes, she was certain it was a confidence problem. Now, that, she could help with.

Alyssa went to check the pitching machine. "You only have two pitches left on this round. I'll comp you ten later if you come outside with me."

He cocked his head. "What's outside?"

She went to the equipment closet outside the cage and pulled down her old softball gear. She kept the glove oiled to toss the ball around with her dad on slow days. It was time to see what Tristan's actual issue was.

Punching her hand into the glove, she looked at him over her shoulder. "Real hitting practice."

Alyssa led Tristan out the back door and down to the small field behind the building. Dad had planned to turn it into an outdoor throwing and catching training facility, but they'd run short on money to put up the nets. Still, Dad kept it mowed, and there wasn't anything Tristan could break if he crushed a pitch.

She was pretty rusty, after all.

She pointed him to the batter's box. It had one of those metal backstops behind it, in case Tristan fouled something off. Hopefully, he wouldn't.

Alyssa held up a softball. "You ever hit one of these?"

He shook his head, looking amused. Uh-huh, he wouldn't here in a sec. She bit back a smirk. "It's been a while since I pitched in a game, but I throw straight and I throw hard. It'll still be about twenty miles per hour slower than the pitchers you'll face."

His forehead scrunched up. "So…why are we doing this exactly?"

"I need to get a feel for you…" She paused, then covered her face with her glove. Her sides quaked with a mixture of total embarrassment and complete amusement. Her mouth… Would it ever *not* run without permission? "For your *swing*."

"That's fine, you can feel me, too, if you want." He laughed. "I'm open to whatever."

I just bet you are. The idea wasn't unappealing, not one bit, but they weren't out in the spring sunshine for a stroll. No, days like this were for batting practice. Taking a deep breath, she lowered the glove. He waggled his eyes at her and flexed a bicep.

Yep, she was done. No chance of recovery. She doubled over laughing, hugging her arms to her stomach. "You are such a complete… You know, I don't have any idea how to finish that sentence. You ready to hit?"

He nodded and stepped into the batter's box, grinning away. "Bring it, Kaplan."

Right, time to work. She rolled her shoulders and held the ball to her glove. Hoping she wouldn't throw way outside, she wound up and threw.

The first ball went straight down the middle, and Tristan stared at her, eyes wide. "Damn. Why don't you play at Suttonville? The softball team hasn't had a solid pitcher for three years."

"I prefer ballet." She smiled, feeling awkward, and gestured at her body. "I know I don't look like much of a ballerina, but I love to dance."

"You look plenty like a ballerina." His eyes raked over her appreciatively. "Especially those legs."

She bit her lip and picked up another softball, almost dropping it because her hands were shaking. How was it that this gorgeous, funny boy had come to flirt with *her*? She wasn't Lauren. She thought guys like Tristan would be collecting "blondes of the week" rather than ogling a girl of average height with crazy-ass hair. "Um, thanks. Now, try hitting this one?"

He smiled at her, teasing. Oh, yeah. Totally flirting. She could get used to this, so long as he didn't play her. Making sure he was ready, she wound up and threw. A little inside but hittable.

Tristan swung hard, and damn if he didn't hit that softball over her head and into the field behind them. He stared at his bat in amazement. "Maybe I should switch to softball?"

"You would've hit a baseball with that pitch, too." She picked up another ball. Time for an experiment. She needed to stress him out. "Who are you playing next?"

"Allen." His shoulders crept up, and his stance went from loose to tight. "They have an all-American pitcher."

"Uh-huh." She wound up before he could finish and threw. Another straight pitch, if a little slower than the other two.

Tristan whiffed it. His hands tightened on the bat like he was trying to strangle it. "Shit."

Nodding to herself, she dropped her glove and walked over to him. She needed to rattle that doubt out of his head. The best way to do that was to throw his mind out into space, and she had an outrageous idea. Totally not like her… Maybe the sun was getting to her.

When they were toe to toe, close enough that she could see variations of brown in his dark eyes, she put her hands on his arms. They were just as strong as she'd imagined, and she had to fight the urge to run her fingers down them. She wanted him off balance, but fondling his forearms seemed like a step too far. Clutching his biceps, she looked him straight in the eye. "Anybody ever tell you how great these arms are?"

Now it was Tristan's turn to flush. "Uh…"

"Hold that thought." She winked at him and swung her hips as she walked back to the pitcher's mound. She heard a low whistle and smiled mischievously. She had him. Without a word, she turned and threw as hard as she could. The pitch flew a little outside, but Tristan got every piece of it. The ball sailed even farther than the first.

Out of softballs, she pointed at him. "You're stressed out. That's your problem."

"I know I'm stressed out." He ran a hand through his hair, making it stand up. "What I can't seem to do is shake it off."

"Hmm." She walked slowly toward him. "You seemed to hit fine when you were focused on me."

He blushed. God, that was cute. "Yeah, I did."

He took a step toward her, and they stopped less than a foot from each other. "Tristan…do you have a girlfriend?"

Shit. Why did she ask him that? *Why?* Another citation

for unauthorized speaking. Mortified, Alyssa covered her mouth with her hands. Tristan laughed and gently pried them loose. "No. Haven't for a while."

"Oh." Her confidence was kind of shot now, but what the hell? She'd come over here for a reason, and after all the bombshells of the last few days, it was time for a little crazy. She *needed* a little crazy. She put her hands on his shoulders and went up on her toes so her face was even with his. His breath was warm on her cheek, and goose bumps raised on her arms. "I have a prescription for your batting troubles."

"Yeah?" he whispered, his eyes glued to her lips.

She smiled.

And kissed him.

Chapter Ten

Holy. Shit. Alyssa was kissing him. Like actually kissing him.

For a second, he was so shocked, he just stood there like a dumbass. Then his brain caught up, and he wound his arms around her and kissed her back. This was the wildest thing that had happened to him in weeks...and he'd helped Kyle fend off a pack of football players over spring break.

Alyssa was warm and soft in his arms. She smelled good, too, like spring flowers and cotton and a little bit of glove oil. Best of all, her hair *was* perfect for running his fingers through, even still in its ponytail. He'd been right about that, and he really loved putting the theory to the test.

He could've gone on kissing her, with the sun warm on his back and the scent of grass in the air, but she stepped away from him, smiling shyly...with a hint of devilry peeking through.

She picked up one of the softballs he'd missed and walked back to the pitcher's mound. His brain was a tangled mess of electricity, and he grabbed his bat out of pure habit more than any real purpose. Before he could even get set, she threw a gorgeous curveball right at him.

He swung, relying on muscle memory, instinct, and a little bit of prayer to the baseball gods. And he *crushed* that ball. It sailed way out into the field…a definite home run.

Alyssa clapped her hands, laughing. Her eyes were alight. "I knew it! Take your mind off the stress of playoffs, and you can still hit. You're getting in your own way."

A little bit of disappointment curled in his chest. "So you kissed me to see if you could get me to hit?"

She walked back to him and patted him on the chest. "Not entirely."

Some of his confidence returned. "So part of you wanted to? To kiss me, I mean."

Her cheeks flushed pink. "Am I weird for kissing you out of the blue like that? Lord. I am, aren't I?"

"Not weird…surprising. Unpredictable." He put a finger under her chin and tilted it up. "Sassy as hell."

She laughed. "I have been accused of sass before."

"I believe it." He couldn't keep his eyes off her mouth. She had these full lips meant for kissing, and he was ready to give it another go, but maybe he should actually ask her out first. Not be the douchebag who made out with a girl but never took her anywhere. "I should repay you for the help. Can I buy you Starbucks when you're off work?"

Alyssa smiled up at him. She wasn't short, maybe five-six, but he'd hit six-one over the summer, so most girls looked tiny. He didn't mind it—she was exactly the right size as far as he was concerned.

She rose on her toes again and pecked him on the cheek. "I'd love that."

Alyssa went after the ball that had gone the farthest. When she found it, she held it up and called, "How far, do you think? About three fifty?"

Three hundred and fifty feet? Tristan turned to look back toward the batter's box. She was right—it was a home run for any high school stadium. That kiss had worked some kind of alchemy on his swing. He smiled as he picked up the other balls. Maybe he should convince Alyssa to come to the playoff games and kiss him right before he went to bat. Picturing the look on Coach's face at that request made him laugh. He could almost hear him say, "Murrell, have you lost your mind?"

Yeah, maybe he had. He glanced up at Alyssa. She was bent over, picking a few wildflowers out of the grass. This girl was herself, and nothing else. That made her pretty much a unicorn, as most of the girls he'd known were too worried about what people thought about them. She stood, a softball in one hand, and a bunch of daisies in the other. When she noticed him looking, she shrugged. "My mom likes them."

Nodding, he trotted into the field. The little white flowers were everywhere, and soon he had a bunch twice the size Alyssa had held up. He took the softball from her and handed her the daisies. "Thanks for helping me out today."

"Thanks for the flowers." She nudged him with her hip, and he swore waves of heat radiated from the spot. "I'm off at four but have a few things to do at home. Want to meet up at six?"

He smiled, getting an idea. Once they exchanged numbers, he said, "Meet me at the ball fields at school. Text me what kind of coffee you want, and I'll bring it."

She looked a little skeptical but smiled. "See you then."

"Definitely."

Alyssa drove up to the stadium right at six. Tristan was waiting for her, standing beside his car with two cups. She'd asked for an iced coffee, black, which wasn't what he'd expected, but he bought it as ordered. Then again, she didn't strike him as a double-mocha latte girl, either.

When she climbed out of her car, his heart skipped. She'd changed into a little skirt and a plain pink T-shirt that went great with her skin. Her hair was loose, curling around her shoulders. Proof that Alyssa could glam it up as easily as she could hit a baseball.

Tristan liked it.

"Here." He held out her coffee. "I wanted to show you something."

She raised an eyebrow. "Should I go back for my pepper spray?"

He laughed. "No." He popped the trunk for a blanket, realizing too late she might not believe him. "No matter how this looks."

"Yeah, sure. Random guy asks me out to a deserted field, tempts me with coffee, and asks me to go somewhere while he's carrying a blanket. There's *nothing* suspicious here." She grinned at him, totally teasing. "Where are we going?"

"Follow me." He led her to a gate near the third baseline. Everyone on the team knew the latch could be jimmied if they wanted to go inside after hours. He wriggled it open, and the gate swung wide. "Head for center field. That's my turf."

"I wondered." She strode across the field, looking as at home here as she did at Swing Away. "I knew you weren't a pitcher."

He caught up with her and spread the blanket out on the grass. "How'd you know?"

She sat on the blanket and patted the place beside her. He sat, and she took his free hand, his throwing hand, and pointed at his fingers. "Wrong kind of calluses. You throw the ball less frequently."

Whoa. "You really know your stuff."

She shrugged. "We see a lot of players. My dad played in the minors for a while before he met my mom. He didn't make the show, so he dropped out, but he taught me a lot, you know?"

Tristan wished he could say yes. His dad wouldn't have even *noticed* the calluses, let alone been able to figure out he was a fielder from them. "Still."

She winked. "That and I might've looked at the team roster on the website earlier."

He laughed. "You got me."

"I really did know about the pitching thing, though." She held up her hands. "Plus, you have a scab on your knee. You dove for something recently, didn't you?"

"I'm going to call you Sherlock if you aren't careful." He looked down, realizing she hadn't let go of his hand. "What about you? It's obvious you love the game. What made you leave it for ballet?"

She took a drink of her coffee before answering. "I love it more. I can't explain it, really. But ballet opens something up inside of me, makes me feel beautiful and strong. Plus, I love moving to music. The grace of it."

She paused, and in the failing light, Tristan noticed her cheeks had gone pink. "I think you'd be beautiful no matter what you did."

She gave him a shy smile. "Are we back to needing the pepper spray? Because that was one hell of a line."

"No, I mean it. You have confidence, and I like that in a girl." He set his coffee down and reached out to brush her hair out of her face. "But, do you always threaten interested guys with pepper spray?"

"No." She toyed with the straw sticking out of her coffee cup. "Just the ones who will put up with a little teasing."

"Oh, good. I was worried there for a second." They sat, quiet, for a moment. The wind had kicked up a little, rattling the chain-link fence around the outfield. "You seem close to your dad."

"I'm close to both my parents." Alyssa scooted to lie down on the blanket, staring up at the sky. "Weird, but true. You?"

"Um…" That was a hard question to answer, especially with a pretty girl stretched out on a blanket next to him. "They're okay. They're both super smart."

"Smart's good." She turned to look at him. "You should see these clouds."

The invitation was plain, and Tristan didn't waste time lying down next to her. The sun had sunk low enough to hide behind the press box, allowing a good view of the sky without Tristan having to shield his eyes. Huge, puffy clouds floated overhead, a few already tinged orange-pink with a hint of sunset. He pointed at one cluster. "That looks like a Mickey Mouse head."

"It does." She scooted closer, so their arms were touching, and it was all Tristan could feel. Her arm against his. "It's pretty out here."

"Yeah. I love it."

"You asked me why I love ballet." Her fingers found his. "Why do you love baseball?"

Tristan drew a deep breath, focused more on the swooping in his stomach than the question. "Uh, the smell. Grass, dirt, leather. I have this vivid memory of the first time I played in a Little League game, how my new glove smelled. How the pants fit, what it was like to wear a baseball cap for the reason they're made for. I liked how it felt to swing and connect, and the thrill of catching a ball to save a play. Some guys would say the best part is winning. Others would say the athletic part. It's more how it makes me feel."

"That's why the swing issues are bugging you so much," Alyssa said. "It's personal, kind of."

"Yeah, I guess that's true."

"What else do you do for fun?" she asked. "It can't be baseball all the time."

He smiled a little, deciding against the answer that had jumped into his head. "I like to water-ski out on the lake. We have a ski boat, even though all my parents do is ride around in it."

"I've never been on a boat."

She didn't sound wistful, but he wondered if he sounded like a well-off snob for having a boat at all. "I'd be happy to take you out sometime."

"I'd like that." She laughed a little. "But the only repayment I can offer is to introduce you to my dog."

"I like dogs." He turned his head to look at her. All he could see was her profile, but it was enough. "Alyssa?"

"Yeah?"

"Would you mind if I kissed you?"

Chapter Eleven

He's adorable. That was all Alyssa could think. He'd *asked* to kiss her, even after she'd simply kissed him without warning earlier. She turned her head to find him watching her. When she looked at him, he propped himself up on one elbow.

Smiling, she nodded. "You have permission."

He laughed at that. "You're a tough cookie."

"I've been told." *Yeah, because* that *is what a guy wants to hear right before kissing a girl*. "Sorry. I have a sarcasm gene. What I meant to say, is, yes—please kiss me."

"See, you say 'sarcasm gene' like it's a bad thing." Tristan tucked some hair behind her ear, and she shivered a little. "I happen to like sarcastic people."

"Thank God," she murmured.

He smiled and bent to kiss her softly. This was different than their earlier kiss. There wasn't any surprise or shock, just sweetness, with a little shyness thrown in for fun, and an edge underneath that promised more. A *lot* more.

The wind gusted, blowing Alyssa's skirt up *way* higher than was appropriate, and she pulled away with a little squawk. "Sorry. The wind's trying to get into my skirt."

Tristan flopped back down next to her. "I paid it to do that."

"Dangerous of you," she said, shaking her fist at the sky. "Both of you."

"Oh, I know my place."

She rolled onto her side and pushed herself up. "And where's that?"

He sat up, too. "Closer to you."

She blushed and stared at the blanket. "Why? You don't know me all that well."

"Let's see. I know you like baseball, ballet, and your dog. Your mom likes daisies. You're close to your dad, and you carry pepper spray in your car—which is a Honda." He reached out to tilt her chin up so they were facing each other. "But I'd like to know you better. Think I could see you at school tomorrow?"

He sounded so tentative, like he was scared she'd run away. She didn't know many cute boys who weren't totally confident in their ability to hook a girl. It was charming. "Definitely."

He smiled, then craned his neck to look up at the sky. It had gotten progressively darker as they'd sat talking. Now he pointed straight up. "First star. It's, uh, actually Venus. But close enough, right?"

She followed his gaze to the silvery dot in the twilight sky. "It counts. Want to wish on it?"

He wrapped an arm around her waist and leaned in to kiss her again. "You make a wish. Mine already came true."

Alyssa decided not to tell Lauren about the date—wait, was it a date? It felt like a date. Either way, meeting Tristan was too new to talk about, and she wanted to keep it to herself. To hold the possible "maybe, if" close like a kitten and enjoy the purr.

Tristan was so funny when he wasn't stressed out, and sweet, too. Based on her dating experience, that was a rare thing. She could get used to it, though. And she hoped she would.

"What's up with you?" Lauren asked at their lockers Monday morning. "You're humming and haven't heard a thing I said."

"What? I heard you." Alyssa flashed a confused smile. "What did you say?"

"I thought so." Lauren rolled her eyes, but she didn't seem mad. "I said today's the day."

"For what?"

"I'm going to talk to that guy I like."

"Good for you." Alyssa meant it, too. Maybe they could double-date sometime. "Take the bull by the horns, or whatever."

"Yes." Lauren smoothed her shirt. "How do I look?"

Today, her friend was wearing a pair of white shorts with a cute blue top that matched her eyes. Her hair swung straight and golden down her back. Alyssa held in a sigh. She'd dressed with more care this morning, too, knowing she'd see Tristan again, but Lauren could wear a paper bag and look gorgeous.

Alyssa snorted. "Perfect, like always."

"Oh, stop." But Alyssa knew Lauren was pleased. "If I haven't worked up the nerve to talk to him by lunch time, you'll give me a shove, right?"

"I will, but you won't need it." She gave Lauren a hug. "Good luck."

...

Tristan

"So?" Dylan asked on the way to their lockers on Monday morning. "You ask that girl out?"

Tristan couldn't stop the smile spreading across his face. "I did."

"And?"

"We went out last night."

Tristan had never seen his best friend so impressed. Both of Dylan's eyebrows went up. "Seriously? I guess that means I need to ask out the girl in history."

Tristan laughed. "Yeah, you do. Look at it this way, when has the lucky polo failed?"

"Never."

"Right." Tristan pointed at it. "You have your lucky glove for games and your lucky polo for asking girls out. Seems to have worked out so far."

After Dylan left for class, Tristan lingered around the lockers, wondering where Alyssa's was. Suttonville was built kind of like a ladder. The senior hall cut across the middle of the school, so the seniors could all be together, but the junior lockers were all along the outer halls, so she could be anywhere. That was the problem with a school this size—with eight hundred students in each class it was hard enough to wade through the crowd to make it to class, let alone find a single girl among the hundreds of people choking the halls.

He'd woken up feeling better than he had in weeks. His muscles felt loose, and the kink that had been building in his neck was gone. Funny how the right person can come along and make everything better.

The morning passed in a haze. Alyssa was at the front of his mind, so x's, y's, past participle Spanish verbs, and the

American Civil War didn't have a chance at breaking through. Finally, it was lunch, and Tristan hurried to the cafeteria, planning to wait for Dylan and a couple other guys from the team, but also be on the lookout for Alyssa. He slowed to a stop when he spotted Dylan outside his history class. He was leaning against the wall, talking to a girl.

He was doing it! He was asking the girl out.

Tristan moved out of the main traffic in the hall, trying to take a closer look. Something about the way the girl was standing was familiar. So was that curly hair…

The air left Tristan's lungs. What was it that Dylan had said? *Amazing green eyes.*

Dylan was asking out Alyssa.

Tristan turned and stalked to the cafeteria, not waiting to find out what happened.

· · ·

ALYSSA

All morning, Alyssa had slowly put her books into her bag, killing time in the hope of seeing Tristan, but Suttonville High was huge, and she never caught sight of him in the crowd. She'd forgotten to ask which lunch he had, so she wasn't even sure she'd see him then. She went from class to class, always on the lookout, with no luck, until her history class finally ended, signaling lunch, and she filed out with the other students. She was preoccupied, still searching, so when a voice piped up next to her, she jumped.

Dylan, a guy she barely knew from history, had appeared out of nowhere. "How's your day been?"

"Uh, fine." Alyssa fought a raising eyebrow. Why had he suddenly decided to talk to her? "Yours?"

"Good. It's good. Um, I've been meaning to ask you something." Dylan cleared his throat, looking nervous. "I was wondering if you'd go out with me for coffee or ice cream at Dolly's sometime after school?"

What was it with guys suddenly realizing she was alive? "Um…I work after school, just about every day."

He flashed her a movie-star smile. He was blond and blue-eyed—like Lauren—and he used it to full effect. "Maybe Sunday? You don't have to give me an answer today. Just think about it?"

She smiled back, not sure what to do. "Okay. I'll, uh, let you know in a few days, once I find out my schedule for Sunday."

And that's a total lie… I work the same hours every single week. Still, she didn't have the heart to outright say no to the guy right off the bat. He seemed nice enough, so she needed time to figure out how to let him down easy.

"Great." His smile took on a relieved note. "See you tomorrow."

Then he was gone, lost in the crowded hallway that led to the cafeteria. Lauren came out of their classroom, eyebrows raised. "What was *that* about?"

"He asked me out." Alyssa gave her friend a helpless shrug. "I have no idea. I haven't said two words to the guy all semester."

"Hmm. That's funny, since I've noticed him watching you for a few weeks now." Lauren winked and sauntered down the hall.

Alyssa hurried to catch up. "And you didn't think to mention it?"

"Guys watch girls all the time and don't do anything about it." Lauren gave her a knowing smile, because she knew all about boys watching her. "I wasn't sure what he was up to."

"You're going to have to tell me what that feels like, because this is my first experience with being covertly watched."

"In class." Lauren's smile turned sour. "Covert watching happens more than you think. Certain creepers have no problem following a girl all around the school."

"Creepers who want to follow me around are liable to get threatened with a baseball bat." Alyssa sighed. This new territory had her rattled. She wasn't the girl guys flocked to.

"Are you going to go out with him?"

It took Alyssa a second to realize Lauren meant Dylan. "Not sure."

"Are you kidding? He's adorable. Live a little." Lauren slung an arm around her shoulders. "Take a walk on the wild side."

"I'll give it some thought…but there's this other guy."

A squeal interrupted anything else Alyssa might've said. "Are you serious? You haven't been interested in anyone in months! Who is he? Where does he live? Is he a student here?"

"Uh…" A flush crept up Alyssa's necks as the students around them in the cafeteria line turned to stare. Lauren wasn't exactly keeping her questions on the down-low. "He's a student here, but I met him at Swing Away."

"A ballplayer? Amazing!" For a second, it looked like Lauren was going to pump her for more information, but she stopped, her mouth snapping shut. "Oh my God, Alyssa. There he is!"

Alyssa tried to see over all the tall people around them. "Who?"

"The *guy*. The one I've been trying to work up the nerve to talk to." Lauren pointed in the general direction of some tables along the windows in the back: Jock Row, as most people called it.

Alyssa forced her way through the crowd to peek at the table. Funny, Dylan was there. "Um, you mean Dylan? If you want him, you can have him."

"No, the *other* one. The cutie with the brown hair and brown eyes. The one laughing."

Oh, sweet baby Jesus…

Tristan.

Alyssa swallowed hard against a sudden wave of nausea. "I know him."

"Yeah? What's his name?"

Lauren's expression reminded Alyssa of an adorable puppy begging for a treat—wide eyes, hopeful smile, the whole thing. "Um…Tristan. His name's Tristan."

"How'd you meet him?" Lauren let out a dramatic sigh. "I've had a crush on this guy forever and come to find out you know him? How's that for luck?"

Yeah, sucky, god-awful, terrible, fate-hates-me luck. "You've had a crush on him forever?"

"Yeah. Well, for a few months, anyway." Lauren grabbed her arm. "So, where'd you meet him? Do you have a class together or something?"

"Or something," Alyssa said, feeling sick. On one hand, Lauren had been her friend since fourth grade and had been dumped by her last two boyfriends in the shittiest ways. One even broke up with her over Snapchat. On the other…the mystery guy was Tristan. Out of the 390-odd boys in their grade alone, Lauren had her sights on *Tristan*.

Alyssa fiddled with the hem of her T-shirt. *How do I get out of this? If I tell her the truth, will she even understand?* She took one look at Lauren's expectant face and knew there was no way to be honest. Not yet, anyway. Lauren didn't handle letdowns well. "I mean, you don't really know him, right? Dylan's nice. Maybe you ought to get to know him. I…I don't think Tristan is really…"

"My type?" Lauren's eyes narrowed. "He's cute, and he seems nice. What's not my type?"

Lauren wasn't bothering to keep quiet, and now at least

twenty people were watching. Alyssa flushed so badly, she felt sweat prickle her nose. "Laur, maybe we should talk about this somewhere else."

"Just tell me, okay?" Lauren lowered her voice. "Wait, does he have a girlfriend?"

"Yes," Alyssa blurted out. *Shit! What am I doing?* "Um, yes. She goes to that private school in Plano."

"You met her, too?" Lauren sounded skeptical...and disappointed.

Alyssa was going to hell anyway for lying to her best friend, so why not go in a handcart? With flames painted on the sides. "Um, no. Tristan just talks about her, is all."

"Oh." Lauren slumped. "Just my luck. Maybe I'll find the right guy in college or something."

"Don't give up." Alyssa felt hollow. How could she do this? A little part of her knew, but she didn't want to admit it: with everything falling apart, Tristan was one bright spot. Lauren was beautiful, had plenty of money, and was a better dancer...so couldn't Alyssa be the one to get what she wanted in this case? Just once? "I'm sure you'll find someone."

And, hopefully, Alyssa could help Lauren find that someone else before she found out about the lies.

Chapter Twelve

TRISTAN

Tristan faked a smile when Dylan sat down at their table. Even after the shock had worn off, Tristan was still caught off guard by seeing Dylan with Alyssa, even if it was probably nothing…

"Guess what! I asked her out!" Dylan said, setting down his tray in triumph. He tapped the table with his fist and grinned at Tristan. "I finally did it."

"That's great." Tristan took a deep breath. "What did she say?"

"That she works a bunch after school, which is totally cool since we have practice all the time. I asked her about next Sunday, and she said she'd think about it."

Think about it. *Think about it?* Heat spread up Tristan's back. Just what was this girl playing at? "So she said yes?"

"Mostly." Dylan frowned. "I think? God, she isn't letting me down easy, is she?"

I sure hope so. Tristan cringed inwardly. Only a total

bastard would get in the way of his friend's crush. Still, how could he have known Dylan was after the girl he'd kissed yesterday? "I don't know. Guess you'll have to see."

They both would.

Tristan pretended to eat while Dylan and the other guys from the team went on about the playoffs. After his "training" session with Alyssa, Tristan hadn't been too worried, but now he could feel tension creeping into his shoulders. This was turning into a real hell of a Monday.

"Hey, I asked you if you were ready to hit against that left-hander from Allen," Dylan said, poking Tristan in the side. "Where'd you go, man?"

"Just thinking." He pushed his tray away. "Yeah, I practice against you all the time. Why wouldn't I be ready?"

The rest of the guys exchanged looks but left it to Dylan to say, "He pitches a ninety-two-mile-per hour fastball. He's going straight into Triple-A after he graduates. Hitting me is difficult, if I do say so myself, but this guy is other-planet hard."

Great, as if he wasn't knotted up inside enough. "Guess we'll see on Friday, then."

When the others started debating how many hits Kyle would get off Allen's pitcher, Tristan gave up trying to pay attention. He scanned the cafeteria, not sure what he was looking for, until he caught Alyssa staring at him from a table four rows over. She gave him a slight smile, so tiny that he doubted even the blond girl sitting next to her noticed.

But he did.

His pulse leapt, and he smiled back—a quick flash, nothing the guys would detect, either. A little secret, just between the two of them. And right then, he knew why she'd told Dylan why she would have to get back to him for coffee. She had other plans.

He winked at her, and she bit her lip, flushing. He half

expected her to point him out to her friend, but she didn't. Fair enough. He didn't want Dylan to see them staring at each other across a crowded cafeteria, either.

This was going to cause some unnecessary drama later, but maybe she'd understand if he said they needed to keep things on the down-low until the playoffs were over. Dylan was pitching against Allen this week, and getting into a huge fight over a girl would throw off his game. Tristan was having enough trouble for the both of them—Dylan needed to stay frosty.

Still, it was hard to hide the spring in his step as he headed to chemistry.

Chemistry. Now *that* was funny.

"I think he's trying to kill us." Jackson flopped on the bench in the dugout to retie a shoe. "I'm a pitcher. I bunt, and I don't steal bases. Speed is not my skill."

Kyle clunked him on the head with his glove. "Yeah, and what if, just once, your bunt *dies* a few feet from the foul line and you have the chance to beat a throw to first? Are you going to tell us then speed isn't your skill when you're out?"

Jackson bared his teeth at Kyle and growled. Tristan raised his eyebrows. This newbie was talking way too much smack for a sophomore called up to varsity because Mark was hurt. Tristan didn't say anything, though. He knew Kyle would take care of it.

And he did. "Coach, I think Morris wants to do a few more sprints. Says he has something left in the tank."

Coach looked at Jackson, who was red in the face and still panting. His eyes flicked to Kyle for a second, then he nodded. "Good idea. Morris, run two more sets for me."

"What?" When the old man didn't back down, Jackson

shot Kyle a sour look and jogged up the steps.

Tristan smiled at the kid's back. "Nice one, Sawyer."

"You have to housebreak them when they first come up." Kyle sat next to him on the bench. "How's your swing coming along? Better?"

"Better-ish, I think." It was true, too. He'd spent all afternoon thinking about Alyssa's coaching methods and trying not to grin like a goofball in class. "Might be coming out of it."

"Good." Kyle patted him on the back and went to check in with the infielders. Tristan wasn't quite sure what had happened to Sawyer—aside from Faith—but he liked this new, talkative, supportive team captain over the swaggering, loner-ish old Kyle.

Dylan took Kyle's place. He had a glum expression. "The more I think about it, the more I think that girl, Alyssa, was letting me down easy."

Tristan's gut tightened. "Maybe."

"Why, though?" Dylan gave him a hurt look. "Am I really that big a loser?"

Tristan had to pretend to tie his shoe to avoid Dylan's eyes. "No, you aren't. She didn't outright say no or laugh in your face. Girls let guys down easy when they're not interested, but still think the guy's okay."

"You'd think I'd know that already." Dylan let out a self-deprecating laugh. "Except this is the first time I've been turned down. Or *maybe* turned down. I don't exactly know."

Tristan rolled his eyes, still focused on retying his shoe—again. "Lucky. I got shot down a bunch before Raina went out with me."

"Well, it sucks." Dylan sighed and grabbed his glove. "Come on. You're up first."

Nerves tickled the back of Tristan's neck as he reached for his bat. "Fine."

"I'll go easy on you. Promise." Dylan smirked.

Uh-huh, right. Tristan went to the batter's box, got set, and waited on the first pitch. A changeup, barely inside the strike zone. He took a swing and missed it.

Dylan pointed at him. "Gotcha."

"Whatever." Tristan reset. "Don't make me wait all day, princess."

Dylan gave him the finger behind his glove so Coach didn't see, then wound up. Another damned changeup. Tristan let that one go by.

"Hit one already!" Dylan called.

"Quit throwing that crap, and I will!"

Dylan didn't waste any time, throwing a wicked curveball. Tristan gave it all he had, but barely nicked the edge of it. Two pitches later, he had yet to hit one.

"Murrell, get out of your own head!" Kyle called from the dugout. "Find some Zen."

Tristan took a deep breath and let his shoulders relax. He built a picture of Alyssa in his mind, the way she smiled, how she felt in his arms, even the way she smelled. Dylan, who'd been watching him, smirked, wound up, and tossed a fastball straight down the middle.

The swing started without Tristan even having to think about it. His entire body followed through.

Ting!

The ball sailed up, up, up, and over the back fence. Kyle let out a whoop, and even Dylan looked impressed. Tristan stared down at his bat. It hadn't betrayed him for once. Maybe his baseball god was a girl with curly hair and a smart mouth.

Fielding practice went fine as always, and Tristan left the field with some actual, honest-to-God confidence. He checked his phone. It was five thirty. If he hurried, he could get to Swing Away before Alyssa left for the day. Seeing her last night hadn't been enough. Like his confidence in baseball, it had been a while since he'd been this interested in pursuing a girl.

Did he feel a stab of guilt knowing Dylan would be unhappy? Yes, he wasn't a complete asshole. But wasn't everything fair in love and war? Dylan hadn't even talked to Alyssa much before today.

Deep down, Tristan knew he was making excuses, and he knew there'd be hell to pay, but a chance to become a "we" with Alyssa was definitely worth it.

He'd pick up the pieces later.

Chapter Thirteen

Alyssa sat cross-legged on the worn concrete floor, pulling apart the pitching mechanism in cage five. A schematic she'd printed out at school sat beside her. Next to that, her phone displayed the manufacturer's troubleshooting site. So far, she'd done six of the eight things they suggested. She had this thought that if she could just *fix* the damn thing—and the bum machine in cage one—Dad wouldn't worry about coming up with the money for this part.

She wiped a hand across her forehead, grimacing when she noticed the grease on the backs of her fingers. She kicked the machine, waving a wrench at its open panel. "Ready for try number seven, you piece of—"

"Do you always love on the pitching machines like that, or is this one special?"

Alyssa didn't turn around, despite the smile tugging its way across her face. So Tristan had come after all. "It's special. A most special piece of non-working crap."

The gate squeaked open behind her, and his footsteps came close. A moment later, he sat next to her on the floor. He was wearing athletic shorts and a gray Suttonville baseball T-shirt with the sleeves cut off. Alyssa almost dropped the wrench. Those arms could make a ninety-year-old spinster feel faint. From shoulders to forearms, with ripped biceps in between, there was almost too much to stare at.

Alyssa cleared her throat. "I wasn't sure how much time I needed to finish this project. I thought it'd be easy, and I'd be up front by now."

Tristan gave her a lazy smile. "I came straight here." He gestured to his clothes. "Sorry I didn't dress up."

His eyes were crinkled at the corners and flicked to her forehead. She sighed. "There's grease on my face, isn't there?"

"A little." He picked up a towel from the pile of random tools she'd grabbed from the storeroom and wiped at a spot above her eyebrow. She felt it all the way down to the soles of her feet. "All better."

"Mm-hmm." She blinked to clear her head. "How was practice?"

A brief frown crossed his face before his smile returned. "I think I found a little Zen. I crushed a fastball and sent it over the fence."

Alyssa gave him a fist bump. "Nice job. I wish I could say my day's been half that productive, but I can't."

"What's up with the machine?" He peered inside the open panel, examining the guts of the pitching mechanism. "Any ideas?"

"Lots of ideas, no solutions." She pushed the access panel back into place and gathered up her tools. "We really need it to work, so I was trying to fix it. I'm not all that great with repairs, though, so it was pointless."

Tristan stood and picked up her tool box before offering her a hand. "Can you call somebody?"

Alyssa looked away. "Yeah, about that... Not really. We're, uh, we might have to close. Not enough business, see, since Top Sports came to town."

Tristan froze. "You're going out of business?"

"Maybe, I don't know." She led him to the storage closet. "I hope not, but we're in the hole and have all these repairs that the city inspector demanded we fix, and we can't."

She set her tools on a shelf and looked up when she heard the door shut. Tristan had followed her inside. Maybe she should've felt all jittery with anticipation about being alone in there with him, but all she felt was sad. And tired. And confused.

Then he said, "You love this place, don't you?"

Tears sprang to her eyes. "I grew up here. This is where I spent most of my weekends when I didn't have dance or softball tourneys. My mom's a nurse practitioner, so she had to work weekends sometimes, and Dad would bring me to work with him. It's like my second home. My third's the dance studio, in case you wanted to know."

She slumped against the wall. The reality of losing Swing Away was becoming crushingly apparent. She couldn't even fix the stupid pitching machines. Before she could stop herself, she choked on a sob and covered her face with her hands.

Tristan was there in seconds, wrapping her up in those strong arms. She knew she'd be embarrassed as hell later for crying all over this cute, sweet guy, but she couldn't hold it in. The front of his T-shirt grew damp under her face, but he didn't let go. He rubbed slow circles on her back, not talking or trying to tell her it'd be all right.

That made it both better and worse. It felt right to admit this to him, to lean on him. Who cared if she'd met him two days ago? Out of nowhere, fully formed, Tristan dropped out of the sky at the moment she most needed someone. And maybe she'd done the same thing for him—he looked better today than he had when she first saw him Saturday. Maybe it really was fate or something. On the other hand, Lauren was going to be so hurt when she found out Alyssa had lied to her. That only made her cry harder.

Finally, she reeled it back in. "S-sorry. That was… Yeah, just so you know, I don't always cry when a cute guy shows up."

"You think I'm cute?" Tristan gave her a devilish grin, and she laughed. "Don't worry about it. You have a lot on your mind."

"True." She scrubbed her cheeks with her hands and wiped her palms on her jeans. "There, all better."

He leaned in and kissed her temple. "All better. Do you want to get out of here? Or do you need to stay and work?"

"Could we go for a walk?" Alyssa needed some air, and a little sunshine wouldn't hurt, either, especially if it highlighted Tristan's arms in all their baseball-player glory. "There's a trail across from the field where we practiced yesterday."

"Sure. Whatever you want." He paused, hesitant. "I hate to ask this, but I…kind of have to. Dylan Dennings… I saw him talking to you today."

"When he asked me out?" Was Tristan worried she was blowing him off? "Yeah, but I didn't say yes. He's a nice guy, but I'm, um, seeing someone else at the moment."

The smile on Tristan's face could've melted snow, but there was a tiny furrow between his eyebrows. "I like that answer. I really, *really* do, but Dylan's my best friend."

"Ah." Alyssa moved past him, uncomfortable. This situation was about to be far more interesting than she liked stuff to be. She pulled open the door and motioned for him to follow her. "Then we should talk while we walk…because it looks like *my* best friend has a thing for *you.*"

Chapter Fourteen

TRISTAN

Tristan looked blankly at Alyssa. "*What?*"

"Yeah. Surprise." She closed her eyes and shook her head, like she was trying to ward off the conversation they were about to have. "Let's go outside. Fresh air might help fix this...thing we've gotten ourselves into."

Thing? Was it a thing? He hoped it was a thing, but she was right—they had a problem. "Okay, let's go."

Alyssa waved to her dad on the way out. He waved back, giving Tristan a shrewd look. Tristan did his best to look respectable...or as respectable as he could in a sleeveless T-shirt he intentionally wore to get Mr. Kaplan's daughter's attention. The man's eyes narrowed, and Tristan scurried out the door.

Once they were outside, crossing the field, Alyssa raised her arms over her head and stretched. The hem of her shirt pulled up, revealing taut, olive skin.

Tristan tripped over his own feet.

She glanced over at him, the corner of her mouth turning up. "You okay there?"

Not exactly. "Yeah. The grass jumped up and grabbed my leg."

"Hmm." She didn't look convinced. His ears were on fire, and that was probably a dead giveaway.

"Fine. I'm a hot mess." He spread his hands wide, grinning at the horrible luck that had brought them together. "And, let's be honest, maybe you are, too."

Oh, for fuck's sake… Could you stop being stupidly honest for one second?

Alyssa laughed, though. "You're right. Maybe that's why it's easy to be around you. We're kind of the same."

The way she said it sounded anything but "easy"— underneath her words, he heard a quiet promise. One that said "us" and "we" and "ours." The air caught in his chest. This girl had him hooked. "I'm glad you didn't punch me for saying it."

"I don't punch people for the truth." She waved for him to catch up. "Now that we're out of my dad's earshot, what are we going to do?"

He stretched out his stride until they were side by side. She pointed at a dirt track disappearing into a thin line of trees winding around a creek. He'd had no idea something like this was out here. "What creek is this?"

"Not a creek. A tributary… Welcome to the Elm Fork of the Trinity River. It's down a lot right now, but when we had that big rain a few springs ago, it came over its bank and halfway up the hill to our ball field."

Tristan glanced over his shoulder. Swing Away sat on a little hill. He hadn't noticed that, either. As they ducked into the shade beneath the trees, he asked, "So, your friend… Who is it?"

Alyssa sighed. "You probably don't know her. She didn't

even know your name until today. It's a random crush, but Lauren takes these thing seriously. She's had her heart broken a few times, so I'm pretty protective of her when it comes to guys."

"Same here…about Dylan, I mean." Tristan rubbed at the back of his neck, warding off the tension headache he could feel building. "Pitchers are divas in their own way, and I'm worried if Dylan finds out I'm with the girl he wanted, it will throw him off."

It sounded like a stupid reason, and most girls would've said so, but Alyssa nodded. "As a former pitcher, I know that's true. Look, I already turned him down."

"Ummm." Tristan winced. "Not exactly. He thinks there's a chance you're thinking about it."

"Crap." Alyssa shook her head. "I'll set him straight… *after* the Allen game, if that's what you think I should do."

Tristan let out a relieved breath. "Thanks. What about your friend? You want to talk to her?"

Alyssa stooped to pick up a rock from the path and threw it into the creek, fork, whatever it was. "I already did. I… God, I panicked. I told her you had a girlfriend."

He couldn't help smiling. "You did, huh?"

She rolled her eyes, but even in the shade, he could see her cheeks turn pink. "I did, but that 'she' went to the private Catholic school in Plano."

He stopped and turned to stare at her. "Alyssa, that's not going to work out well. For either of us, or Lauren."

"I know." She took a step forward and bent so the crown of her head rested against his chest. "I don't know what to do. I tried to tell her you weren't her type, and she started getting all pissed at me. We're prepping for auditions for this summer dance camp in Dallas. She's high-strung, just like Dylan, but she's been my friend for years." Alyssa looked up at him with pleading eyes. "Usually I'll let her get her way, because I'm not so hung up about things and I don't want her to be hurt. But, this time… I like hanging out with you. I like *you*. And for once, I'm not going to step aside and let Lauren have her way."

The wistful sound to her voice made him stand up a little taller. *This time*, she'd said. He slid an arm around her waist. "You say that like I don't have a choice."

Alyssa snorted. "She's tall, long-legged, slim, with straight blond hair and blue eyes. You *don't* have a choice."

He tightened his arm around her waist. "What if I like curves, curly hair, and a girl who can throw a fastball?"

She went still. "You do?"

Her voice—she sounded so skeptical. He put a finger under her chin and lifted her head. "Yep. You don't give yourself enough credit, I think. You're hot and confident— which is hot on its own—and you care about things I like. I'd give anything for my parents to enjoy baseball. Your dad owns *batting cages*, and you work there. Hell, when I saw you wielding that wrench earlier…."

She bit her lip, and her eyes were shining. "You get turned on by girls using tools?"

"When certain girls do…" He brushed his lips across her forehead. "Oh, yeah, I do."

"Next time you come to Swing Away, I'm going to wear my tool belt, then. Try to control yourself."

"You have a tool belt?" He grinned down at her. "That's it, I'm going to marry you."

She laughed. "Can we wait until we're twenty-five first?"

"Sure." He leaned closer. "How about I kiss you instead?"

"How about you do that," she whispered, and her eyes fell closed.

He kissed her, softly at first, while the Elm Fork burbled behind them and the leaves rustled. She was so warm and fit against him like she was made to be there. He tangled his free hand in her hair, deepening the kiss, pulling her closer. Right now, it was hard to care about Dylan's feelings, or Lauren's. Alyssa was the only person who mattered.

Even if it came back to bite him later.

She pulled away. "Are you sure about this? Hiding from our friends?"

He took her hand and started walking down the trail again. A couple of lovesick frogs sang the song of their people, and he knew how they felt. He wished he could tell everyone about this great girl he met, but he'd keep it quiet—for a while. It wasn't a bad thing, keeping it to themselves. In a way, they could keep it perfect, without intrusion, at first. "I'm sure. As long as you are."

She leaned into him. "You know what? I am."

He squeezed her hand. "Good enough for me."

Ignoring that little twinge of guilt wouldn't be all that hard, right?

Chapter Fifteen

Alyssa

Tristan left a few minutes before closing time. He didn't do any batting practice, but she imagined his arms were pretty sore after the last few days' work, and he shouldn't overdo it. No matter how much she wanted to watch those arms in action.

Humming to herself—Vivaldi, funny enough—Alyssa finished cleaning up the snack bar. Should she feel bad for lying to Lauren? Probably, but she was too happy. Lauren had *everything* going for her, and guys orbited around her all the time. Missing out on this one wouldn't be terrible for her in the long run. Alyssa giving up a chance with Tristan would be.

Once she was done working, she went to find her dad. He was in his tiny office, sorting receipts and frowning. He looked up when she knocked. "Hey. Are we all shut down for the evening?"

"Yep."

"So, who's the kid?" he asked, giving her a teasing smile.

"Looked like a ballplayer, if I'm not mistaken."

Alyssa blushed. Her dad hadn't had much call to ask that question over the last year. "His name's Tristan. He's on the baseball team at school."

"I've seen him three days in a row now." Dad pointed a pen at her. "Something tells me he's not here to use the cages."

Alyssa squirmed a little under his gaze. "Yeah, about that. We just started getting to know each other, so if you and Mom could avoid making a prime-time story out of it, I'd appreciate it."

"Say no more." Dad dragged a few more receipts—or maybe bills—over to the stack he was working on. "I won't scare him off just yet."

"Please don't." She glanced at the growing pile of paper. "Dad…I wish you'd take my dance money. I probably won't need it."

Not only because she probably wouldn't make the cut, but also because she couldn't imagine going if Lauren was pissed with her. Which she probably would be. Could Alyssa make her understand somehow?

"Chickadee, I'm not taking your money." He gave her a tired smile. "You work so hard, you deserve a little fun. Your mother and I will figure all this out."

Nope, you're not going to blow me off. I'm part of this. "And if we don't?"

Dad took off his glasses and rubbed his eyes. "Then we close the old girl down, and I take an assistant manager position at Top Sports."

Alyssa's jaw dropped. "*Top Sports?* You'd sell out?"

Dad groaned. "I told Mom you'd take the news like that. 'Dee, they offered me a job, probably to encourage me to shut down, kind of like when Whole Fitness came to town and bought up the two local gyms."

"You can't take the job." God, she was so angry her hands

shook. "You *can't.*"

"It's not like I want to." Her dad's voice rose, warning her not to push too far. "But we have to have a roof over our heads without your mother working herself to death. You need money for college. And, just so you know, I told them if I went to work there, you had to be offered a job, too, with flexible hours and immediate seniority. Lord knows you deserve it, working here all these years."

Work at Top Sports? Leave Swing Away and work for the enemy? Tears filled Alyssa's eyes. "I'm going home."

Her dad heaved a sigh as she turned around. "I'll be there as soon as I can."

Alyssa was too upset to say good-bye. She fled to her Honda and climbed inside. It grumbled and choked and threw a little fit before starting, and she rested her head on the steering wheel. This day…this crazy, horrible, wonderful, terrible day. She lifted her head to look at the business's sign.

SWING AWAY: BATTING CAGES FOR LEAGUES BIG OR SMALL.

The sight of it made her heart ache.

Not sure what tomorrow would bring, Alyssa drove home.

After washing the dishes so her mother wouldn't have to, Alyssa sat on her bed working on her French homework. The words kept blurring together on the page of her textbook. Her parents were talking downstairs, and she itched to know what they were discussing. But she'd overstepped with Dad this afternoon—she knew that now—and she decided to let them work things out without her opinions. They didn't want her money, and there was no other way she could help.

Exhausted, she slammed the book closed and reached for her phone. Lauren had sent her three texts.

L: *Okay, I need your help.*

L: *Right, you're at work. Text me tonight.*

L: *Yoohoo!*

Alyssa swiped her screen. *Here now. What?*

L: *Yay! I have an idea, and I need your help.*

A: *With what?*

L: *Operation Tristan.*

Alyssa stared at her phone. This wasn't good. Not even a little bit.

A: *What do you mean? Isn't he taken?*

Yes, yes, he was.

L: *That's what I mean. Operation break Tristan up with his girlfriend.*

A: *Not nice, Laur. You aren't like this.*

L: *She's not even in school with us. I'm not saying we lie to him. Just help me tempt him a little.*

Alyssa's blood boiled. Their whole lives, Lauren had taken Alyssa for granted, sure she'd follow wherever Lauren led. Now she wanted Alyssa to help her break up Tristan and his girlfriend? So what if the girlfriend was fake—kind of? This was a low thing to do. And if she was this far gone, what was she going to do if she found out the truth?

A: *No. Count me out.*

The screen stayed blank for several minutes. The little dots saying Lauren was typing a reply didn't come up, either. Alyssa glared at her phone. Silence was not golden where Lauren was concerned.

Finally:

Fine. I'll do it myself. He'll be mine before the end of school. Count on it. Dylan's his friend, by the way. I talked to him after school, and he's going to introduce me. I think he wants me to set you up with him in return, so don't blow him off.

Okay, this wasn't going to end well....at all.

A: *Pls don't do this. This goes from mischief to mean girl. I'm serious. You're crossing a line, and it could backfire big time.*

L: *I'm not asking you to help if you don't want to. Just don't get in the way, all right?*

Alyssa sat back against her headboard and pressed a hand to her eyes. Should she just admit *she* was the competition? And if she did, would Lauren tell Dylan and screw up the team's chances against Allen? No telling what Lauren would do when she found out.

Besides, her best friend was behaving like a lovesick criminal mastermind: *"Just watch, he'll be mine."* Cue the dramatic music and perfectly timed thunderclap.

Alyssa steeled herself against what came next. Let Lauren play her game. Tristan had been pretty clear about what he wanted, and that was *her*, not Lauren. If her friend was going to go off the deep end, no matter what Alyssa said, there was no stopping her.

A: *Fine, whatever. I'm going on the record—this is a bad idea. But I know you'll do it anyway.*

L: *I'm already there.*

Alyssa sat up. *What do you mean?*

L: *I'm at Snap's with Dylan. Tristan is on his way. Oh, I mean here! He's here! God, I gotta go.*

Lauren was meeting Tristan tonight? At Snap's? How'd that even... Alyssa groaned.

She pulled up Tristan's number, thinking she'd text him and tell him it was an ambush, but stopped. Telling him about it felt desperate, like she was jealous and guarding her turf or something. That wasn't her. What happened, happened, and if she couldn't trust Tristan now, what was the point of getting more involved?

Alyssa put her phone under her pillow and dragged her French textbook back out, determined to do some homework and not think about what was happening at Snap's.

Chapter Sixteen

TRISTAN

Monday was meatloaf night at home, assuming Mom wasn't doing late rounds. Dad would be teaching a graduate class, which meant Tristan would be on the hook for eating a double helping. Not. Happening. Just as he was thinking about texting Dylan to go out for dinner, Dylan beat him to it.

D: *Come to Snap's. Dinner's on me.*

T: *Perfect timing, see you there.*

Tristan ran home long enough to put on some jeans and a shirt with actual sleeves, because his favorite server wouldn't enjoy sweaty workout clothes in her section, and he didn't want his Snap's visitation rules revoked. When he ran back downstairs, the smell coming from the kitchen—a cross between burnt rubber, ketchup past its expiration date, and onions...*lots* of onions—convinced him sneaking out for dinner was the right answer.

Which was confirmed as he hurried to the front door. Mom called, "Um, Tristan? I know you're going out. Bring me back a salad, would you?"

Biting back a laugh, he said, "Sure thing. I'll even remember dressing on the side."

There was a relieved sigh, and he bounced out the door, shaking his head and chuckling. His mother could do a quadruple bypass in less than five hours, but meatloaf was *not* her area. He appreciated the effort but wished she would give it up in favor of those fancy prepackaged meal-delivery service things with instructions that said, "Combine this, bake for twenty minutes. The end."

On the way to meet Dylan, he tried to think of a way to keep the topic off Alyssa. He hated to lie, but it was for the best. Dylan had once let things go so badly during a game with McKinney that he'd loaded the bases on the first three batters, then gave up a grand slam, all because he'd gotten a D on a calculus exam. He was so Type A, everything had to be chill for him to perform. Finding out his best friend was betraying him with the girl he liked would spell an end to their playoffs…and Tristan's poor batting wouldn't be the cause. He'd still be at fault, though, and he couldn't do that to the team.

Tristan pulled into the lot next to Dylan's car and trotted inside. Snap's was dimly lit, allowing the twenty-four TVs playing various sports to provide most of the light. He scanned the restaurant the best he could but didn't see a table with a guy alone. Dylan had to be here… Where was he?

"Hey! Over here!"

Tristan's head whipped left, back to a section he'd already looked at, and he realized why he hadn't spotted Dylan. A cute blonde was sitting at the table with him. A little flare of hope flickered to life inside Tristan's chest—maybe Dylan was already over Alyssa.

Nodding, he made his way to the table, dodging a server with a tray full of burgers. "Sorry about that. I didn't realize we'd have company." He smiled at the girl as he took a seat. "I'm Tristan."

She smiled, showing off even, white teeth. Now that was a smile to launch a thousand guys for sure. Dylan had done well.

Then she said, in a soft, throaty purr, "Hi, Tristan… I'm Lauren."

Tristan blinked, then looked at Dylan. Was this a setup? Goddamn it. "Nice to, uh, nice to meet you. So…if I'm a third wheel, I don't mind bouncing. I didn't mean to intrude."

Lauren laughed. Her laugh was completely opposite from Alyssa's. When Alyssa laughed, you felt it. She wasn't afraid to let it burst right out. Lauren laughed like Marilyn Monroe—breathy and with an invitation attached. "You aren't intruding. Actually, Dylan and I have a class together, and we were working on some things. Right, Dylan?"

Dylan nodded, a smirk on his face. "Yep. Oh, and Lauren's *Alyssa's* best friend. Remember me telling you about Alyssa?"

God, did he ever. "Yeah, I do."

He was saved from having to ask what the hell was going on because Kathy appeared at his right elbow. "Well, well, my boys are hosting a friend." She pointed her pen at them. "Use your utensils tonight."

Dylan rolled his eyes. "We aren't that bad."

"Hmm." Kathy shrugged. "What can I get you?"

Tristan and Dylan ordered burgers—if Tristan was going to be trapped in an ambush, he was going to eat something—and Lauren ordered a salad with no dressing.

"None?" Kathy frowned. "A *dry* salad?"

Lauren flashed her killer smile. "I'm watching my figure. I'm a dancer."

"If you say so."

Tristan choked back a laugh. The suspicious tone in Kathy's voice matched what he was feeling. He was sorry to see her go, to lose that buffer. He sipped his Coke and tried not to squirm as Lauren watched him with a predatory stare.

"So, Tristan," she said, leaning forward on her elbows. "You're an outfielder?"

Lauren had chosen her pose with care—her breasts strained at her T-shirt, an outspoken bid for attention. Tristan kept his eyes firmly on hers. "Yes."

"Wow. So, what do outfielders do?" She batted her eyelashes. "I want to learn more about baseball."

Tristan almost groaned. Was she serious? "I catch long drives. Have to run around a lot. That kind of thing."

"Sounds interesting. I was thinking of going to your game against Allen. My friend Alyssa will come with me." She shot Dylan a coy smile, and he winked back.

What, did they think he was totally fooled by this show? "I hope you enjoy the game."

And that's how it went for the next fifteen minutes. Lauren would ask him a leading question, trying to make him talk, and he'd answer her in as few words as possible. Dylan picked up the conversation a lot, sounding more and more frustrated by the lack of progress.

Finally, Kathy brought their food, and Tristan stuffed his face to keep his mouth full. Lauren gave him a puzzled look over her rabbit-food dinner but didn't try to draw him out anymore. He had a feeling this wasn't over, though. Alyssa's bestie struck him as a very, *very* determined girl. He could see what Alyssa meant about letting Lauren get her way. That would be a requirement for a friendship with Lauren…and probably for boyfriends, too.

No, thank you.

When the check came, Dylan picked it up, looking a little

sheepish. "My turn to pay."

Yeah, Dylan owed him for sure. Lauren didn't offer to help cover hers, and Tristan ground his teeth. How was Alyssa patient enough to be this girl's friend? If you looked up either "spoiled" or "entitled" in the dictionary, Lauren would be there, smiling back at you.

He needed to get out of here, so he'd have to order Mom a salad somewhere else. A salad with *dressing*, even if it was on the side. Lauren was classically pretty, long and lean, but Tristan wasn't fooled by the packaging. And that whole dry-salad thing was just for show.

"Thanks, man," he said to Dylan. "I need to run. Mom's expecting me to bring her a salad from Sprout's."

Dylan gave him the first real smile of the night. "Did Meatloaf Monday experience failure?"

Tristan nodded. "Epic. Thanks for dinner." He gave Lauren a passing glance. "Nice to meet you."

Then he turned his back on them and walked out without looking back.

Chapter Seventeen

Alyssa

An hour after Lauren's texts, Alyssa gave up on her homework. She'd pulled her phone out no less than a dozen times, hoping to hear from Tristan… No such luck. She hated that it was bothering her so much. Her self-promise to chill had crashed and burned seconds after she made it.

Grumbling, she went to the bathroom down the hall to brush her teeth and wash her face. What was Lauren thinking? Why did this guy have to be the one to send her over the edge into crazy stalker-girl?

She went back to her room, wondering if eight thirty was too early to go to sleep, and caught sight of her phone — there were text notifications. She snatched it up, feeling a little humiliated at how eager she was for news.

The first was from Tristan.

So, Lauren ambushed me at dinner tonight. Dylan brought her. They're conspiring.

She blew out a breath. The word "ambush" made her less worried. He didn't sound happy, which mean Lauren's spell-work hadn't been successful.

A: *She texted me from the restaurant right as you walked in. Sorry for not warning you—I was worried they'd see I was texting you.*

T: *It's fine. Can I ask you a question?*

A: *Sure.*

T: *So...Lauren. She's a little...God, I'm going to sound like an asshole, but she's kind of spoiled.*

Alyssa laughed.

Nail on the head, first try. Stuffed panda bear to the winner.

T: **snort* So, how are you friends? Or, better question: why?*

That was a good question some days.

We've been friends forever. She wasn't always like this, but when her parents divorced when she was in seventh grade, they fought over her by giving her whatever she wanted in order to be the "favorite." Now she believes the hype. She's a great friend, she just has some issues. We all do. Plus, she's beautiful. That opens a bunch of doors.

T: *Ah, okay. Anyway, can I see you tomorrow?*

Alyssa smiled at the phone. He still wanted to hang out with her—this little drama hadn't changed that. *Yes. Same time tomorrow? I promise not to have grease on my face.*

T: *And wear that tool belt. See you then.*

Alyssa jumped off her bed and did a happy dance. Even if everything else was shit, it would be okay now.

Her phone buzzed again. Alyssa stopped dancing and sighed—it was Lauren.

L: *Well, I met him. He's very cute.*

Alyssa rolled her eyes. *Uh-huh. How'd it go?*

L: *Great! He was very sweet. We talked about baseball and school and everything. I think I made an impression.*

Alyssa stared at the phone. Based on Tristan's reaction, she'd imagined a dinner of awkward. Was Lauren seeing what she wanted to see, or had Tristan been too nice to shut her down? Either way, this spelled trouble.

A: *Are you seeing him again?*

L: *Oh, you know I will. Take me to the game with you on Friday. I need to see him in action, up close.*

Alyssa flopped onto her bed and buried her face in her pillow. Really?

A: *I thought you didn't enjoy baseball?*

L: *I'll learn to. He's worth it, I can tell.*

Tristan *was* worth it, but holy hell, how was Alyssa going

to get out of this alive? Lauren might not speak to her ever again. Even if her best friend was infuriating sometimes, she was still her best friend, and she'd stuck with her through thick, thin, awful hair days, and dance recitals.

Guilt settled into Alyssa's stomach. Was she the one being a terrible friend?

A: *Okay, we can go. I'll teach you the basics while we're there.*

L: *THANK YOU! Love you bunches!*

Alyssa sent a kissy-face emoji back and put her phone on the nightstand. No matter what happened, she had to take care of Lauren. But could she do that and not break her own heart in the process?

She crawled into bed, hoping sleeping on it would make things clearer.

"The server was so rude, making fun of my salad," Lauren was saying. "I could tell Tristan disapproved, but he was too polite to say anything."

Alyssa rubbed at her temples. Lauren had been giving her the play-by-play since first thing that the morning. She'd thought she'd heard the whole story, but here they were at lunch, and there was still more to tell.

"He sounds like a nice guy," Alyssa murmured. She needed to change the subject. "Hey, when do you want to practice next? I'll ask Madame Schuler if we can book the small studio."

Lauren didn't answer. She was staring across the cafeteria, eyes wide. Alyssa followed her gaze and had to hide a smile. Tristan and Dylan were in the lunch line, joking around with a few other guys. They were all laughing and talking with their hands. It was adorable, really.

Tristan looked away from the group, and his eyes swept the crowd until they met hers. He winked, and a flush crept up Alyssa's neck.

Lauren grabbed her arm. "Oh my God. He just winked at me."

Alyssa didn't look at her. "Maybe he has something in his eye."

A napkin hit Alyssa in the shoulder. "You're ruining my flow, girl."

"Sorry." Alyssa threw the napkin back at Lauren, who caught it, smiling. "I know you like him, but could we talk about practice now?"

"Fine, fine." Lauren pulled her phone and a little notebook out of her bag. "I can do tonight and Thursday. Wednesday's out—going to get a pedi with my mom. Will that work?"

Alyssa paused. "Um, I can't tonight, but Thursday's fine."

"What's going on tonight?" Lauren put her notebook away. "Are you working late?"

"Yeah." Alyssa wished she could tell Lauren she had plans, but that would lead to awkward questions. "I'm doing maintenance on the pitching machines."

"I understand."

She prattled on about dance technique for the next ten minutes. Whenever she looked away, Alyssa caught Tristan's eye again. It was so strange to be in a room full of people who had no clue while she felt like she was alone with him. Dylan elbowed him in the side and nodded toward Alyssa. She turned to look at the table, realizing how easy it would be to get caught.

Part of her *wanted* to be caught. To let the secret fly, so she could sit by Tristan at lunch without causing a scene. Frustration welled in her chest. How'd she get herself into this?

"I think I'm finished," she said as Lauren wrapped up a dissertation on the proper angle of an arabesque. "I'll see you in sixth period, okay?"

Lauren waved at her. "Sure. I'm going to stay and work on my trig homework."

Alyssa tossed her trash and made her way outside. There was a patio behind the cafeteria where students could hang out until fourth period bell, but it was almost always empty. The sun was strong today, and a stiff westerly breeze toyed at her hair, blowing it into her face. Tiny puff clouds floated across the sky. There was a charge to the air, though, and in the spring that meant a thunderstorm was coming.

She stood alone for a few minutes but wasn't surprised when a shadow covered hers.

"Hey." Tristan's voice was soft in her ear.

"Hey," she said, not turning around. This was dangerous, but she knew he'd felt a pull inside as much as she had. "We're not exactly invisible out here."

"I know. There's an alcove to the right. I'm going in there. Wait a minute, then follow me?"

Alyssa's heart surged. "I'd love to."

Chapter Eighteen

TRISTAN

The alcove to the right of the patio was the best-kept secret at Suttonville. It was just a little walled-in cubby, nothing much, but it was hidden from the cafeteria's view. Tristan and his ex had sneaked back here on more than one occasion. It had probably been used to hold some kind of equipment at one time, but now it was a ten-by-ten square of near invisibility.

Still, this wasn't the smartest thing to do. Not with the poor excuse he'd given Dylan—"I need to stretch my legs before class"—and Lauren still sitting at a table not far from the windows. But when he'd seen Alyssa leave, a tug had brought him to his feet not two minutes later. Maybe it was the thrill— or the relief—of possibly being caught. Maybe it was the sight of her curly hair, glowing with red highlights in the sun.

Maybe he was just desperate to see her after all the drama last night.

He leaned against the wall facing the little archway and smiled when she ducked inside.

She looked around at the walls, nodding, before flashing him a coy grin. "I had no idea this was even here."

"That's the point." His pulse sped up as he pushed off the wall. "I needed to see you."

She walked over slowly, stopping just short of touching him. "Same."

"I hate that we can't be open about this." He wrapped an arm around her waist and pulled her close. Her hair smelled like spring flowers, and it was soft against his cheek. "Does it make me a bad person to want something I have to hide?"

"We won't have to hide it forever." Her breath tickled his neck. "Just until after Allen."

But it wouldn't be just after Allen—if they won, Dylan would be on tap to pitch again in the state championship game. God, Tristan was such an asshole for not telling her that, but he hoped she'd understand if they won the game on Friday. "We might lose our friends over this… Are you willing to risk it for a guy you've known less than a week?"

She looked up at him, and her eyes caught him. That green could hypnotize a serpent. "There are some people you just *know* after two days, and there are others you realize you never did after ten years. I love Lauren, but the last several months… I'm probably being petty, but I feel like she wants me around to be her shadow or her mirror or something. As long as it's about her, or something related to things she likes, we're fine. But, for once, I want this to be about *me*. Is that terrible?"

Tristan kissed her temple. "Not even a little bit. Dylan's been a great friend to me, and a teammate, so this is harder. Still, I totally understand what you mean about knowing someone right off." He gave her a goofy grin. "You're good people, Alyssa Kaplan."

She leaned her head against his shoulder and chuckled against his collarbone. "That sounded like something my

Meemaw would've said. But…" She grinned up at him. "You're damn good people yourself, Tristan Murrell."

Willing the bell not to ring and put an end to things, Tristan brushed her lips with his, and she responded, hungrily. With his first girlfriend, it had been weeks of flirting before they even went out. That had been a special relationship, but this was entirely different. Alyssa lit him on fire, made him want to climb a mountain just to show off for her. Maybe this is what a soulmate was—someone who got you, right away, and made you want to spend every waking minute with that person, no matter how hard it would be.

And he damn well would…as soon as he could figure out how to let Dylan down easy.

"So… Guh, just a second." Dylan panted for breath. Coach had run them through sprint drills right after warm-ups, and no one had their wind back yet.

"Don't…try to…talk." Tristan sank onto the bench in the dugout and put his head between his knees to ward off the dark spots behind his eyes.

"You guys need to jog more during the off-season." Kyle Sawyer strolled by, barely sweating. "Work on that lung capacity."

Tristan grimaced and flipped him off. Good-naturedly, but still. The guy was a beast.

Kyle laughed and patted him on the head. "Awww, should I call your mommy?"

"Shut up, Sawyer." Tristan gave him the eye. "Bad air today, that's all."

Kyle frowned and looked at the sky. The wind at lunch had died, leaving an oppressive, humid afternoon behind— the kind of afternoon that sparked ozone alerts and calls for inhalers. "You know, I think there's a storm on the way."

If Kyle said it, it was truth. Tristan was still having trouble wrapping his head around the fact that Kyle was a landscaping genius, but his own parents' lawn—they were new customers—didn't lie. Tristan sat up and eyed a dark smudge on the horizon. "You might be right."

If it stormed, practice would be called early…which meant he could meet up with Alyssa sooner. "I hope it does rain."

Kyle raised an eyebrow. "We need the practice, dude."

"Um, yeah." Tristan grabbed his glove for fielding practice. "You're right. I'm just tired or something."

Kyle continued to watch him as they jogged across the field to their positions. "Sure you're okay? Your hitting seems to be coming back some."

"Some." Tristan caught the ball from second base and threw it to Kyle.

"You're doing fine. Don't worry about it. We've got what it takes." Kyle threw the ball back. "And Dylan is going to smoke Allen. He looks great."

It was true—Dylan did look great, determined and ready to kick ass. Guilt clawed up Tristan's throat. "I think so, too."

Except, while Dylan looked good, his fastball left Tristan swinging at air, and increasingly frustrated. Even when he tried to think about Alyssa, he couldn't hit a damn thing. It wasn't just bad head space—the guilt was choking him off from whatever part of his brain controlled hitting. He stalked down to the dugout and traded his aluminum bat for a wooden one.

"Dude, settle down!" Dylan yelled when he came back to the batter's box. "You're supposed to be coddling me, not the other way around."

Tristan sighed and stepped back into the batter's box. He could feel every eye in the dugout on his back. He shifted his stance and centered his weight.

You're thinking too hard, a voice remarkably like Alyssa's murmured in his head. *Try again.*

He let out a slow breath as Dylan wound up. Another fastball, eighty-five-plus miles an hour. Tristan let his arms move without forcing it. *Crack!*

The ball flew to left field, dropping into the corner—a stand-up double. Tristan let himself relax, and his arms shook. Nerves, adrenaline, who knew? It felt good to make contact, though.

"Good one!" Dylan gave him a thumbs-up. "Let me torture someone else, yeah?"

Tristan waved at him and jogged back to the dugout. Kyle eyed him shrewdly. "What came over you out there?"

"Nerves, I guess." Tristan shoved his bat into his equipment bag and dropped onto the bench next to Kyle.

"No, when you *hit* the ball." Kyle jerked his chin toward home plate. "Your whole stance changed. You loosened up, centered your body, the whole thing. What did you do to fix it?"

Tristan bent to dig in his bag to avoid eye contact. "Just thought about something other than baseball, I guess."

Not strictly true, but true enough. He sat up to find Kyle giving him an odd look. "Who is she?"

"What?" Tristan's heart started beating an unsteady rhythm. "I don't know what you mean."

"Look, I was good before Faith showed up, but…" Kyle gave him a cocky smirk. "But we both know I'm pretty awesome now."

Tristan took his time pulling off his batting gloves, wondering how Kyle knew. And if he knew, how long before Dylan suspected something? "You were already awesome."

"Yes, but I'm *more* awesome. Being with her took the edge off, you know?" To Tristan's surprise, Kyle blushed.

The dude *blushed.* "Having her around makes me better at everything."

There was a slight hitch on the word "everything," and Tristan stared at him. In the past, Kyle hadn't stuck with a girl for more than a few days, far as Tristan knew, yet he'd been with Faith for a while now, and it was clearly making an impact.

Alyssa had already done the same for him.

Tristan glanced at Dylan, who was trash-talking their first baseman from the mound. Could Kyle keep a secret? Tristan needed to talk to someone, someone who'd tell him if he was being an idiot or not. He motioned Kyle closer. "There is a girl. I met her last weekend, but I'm crazy about her. She, uh, she knows a few things about baseball, too."

Kyle cocked his head. "Okay, who is it? And why are you acting like this is a state secret?"

Tristan glanced back at the mound. The pitching coach was up there now, talking to Dylan. "Because Dylan likes her. I had no idea she was the girl he wanted to ask out until after *I* did."

Kyle let out a low whistle. "That's not good."

"I know! I don't want to upset him before the game. Luckily, Alyssa understands—"

"*Alyssa*? As in Faith's friend, Alyssa?" Kyle leaned back against the dugout, a pained expression on his face. "Do you know her other friend, Lauren, likes you?"

"Um, yeah."

"Okay, that's a mess," Kyle said. "Can I tell Faith? I think she was going to try to set Lauren up with you."

Tristan pinched the bridge of his nose. "Tell me this isn't happening."

"What's not happening?"

Tristan's head whipped around to find Dylan standing right behind him. He didn't look suspicious or pissed, so maybe he hadn't heard anything. "That, um, Kyle thinks I have a hitch in my swing for real."

Kyle shot him a pointed look but nodded. "He'll get over it, but he's going to have to *work out his issues.*"

Dylan looked between them, forehead wrinkled in confusion. "Um, okay. Sorry about that, man."

A rumble of thunder put a stop to any more awkward questions. Coach was calling the second string in from the field, and a dark gray cloud was rolling slowly toward them.

"That's it for today." Coach peered up at the sky, looking like he was about to shake his fist at the cloud. "Only good news is Allen is probably going to be rained out, too."

"But they have an indoor facility to practice in," Dylan muttered. Then he paused. "What about the batting cages?"

"At Top Sports? Those are outside," Kyle said. "No-go there."

"No, what about that old place just outside of town? Maybe they're open—it's indoors."

Kyle shrugged and glanced at Tristan. "You want to come?"

Tristan's insides had frozen over. He was so flipping stuck, all he could do was nod. This was going to be a disaster... but there was no way he was letting Dylan go to Swing Away alone. No way in hell.

Chapter Nineteen

ALYSSA

The steady thrum of heavy rain on Swing Away's metal roof always gave Alyssa a sense of contentment. It reminded her of rainy Sunday afternoons, hanging out with her dad and learning to watch pitches. Even better, the rain would mean baseball practice was over, and Tristan would be here soon to take her out.

On that thought, Alyssa grabbed her phone. Tristan had texted all right, but not with the news she expected.

T: *Half the team is headed your way, Dylan included.*

T: *I'm coming, too, but they want to do batting practice. Does he know where you work?*

Alyssa chewed her lip. The texts were fifteen minutes old—the guys would be here any minute. She didn't think Dylan knew she worked here, but that was about to change.

Shit!

She jogged to Dad's office. "We have incoming. Sounds like half the Suttonville baseball team is on the way to do batting practice. Their practice was rained out."

Dad's reading glasses dropped out of his hand onto the desk. "You're kidding. Quick, we need to make sure all the machines are fully loaded."

Her dad popped up and took off for the cages. Alyssa forced herself to breathe and followed. She started from the back and had filled cages six, seven, and eight before the bell at the door began jangling wildly.

"They're here!" Dad called, before dashing up front.

Alyssa wiped her sweaty palms on her jeans and smoothed back her hair. Was Tristan going to acknowledge her existence, or were they going to play it as strangers?

When she rounded the corner, though, the first person she ran into was Kyle. He leveled a curious look at her. "Your dad said I'm in cage eight. Can you show me?"

He was standing under the cage three sign, clearly on his way down there. But the seriousness in his gaze had her nodding. "Sure, right this way."

She walked him to the back corner and was about to show him where the tokens went, but Kyle pulled her aside. "Look, I know about you and Tristan. I'm going to do my best to talk Faith out of helping Lauren, but—"

"Helping Lauren?"

He sighed. "She's working on me to set Lauren up with Tristan for a double date. I'm going to wave her off, but I might have to tell her why. I wanted you to know before I did anything."

How does he even know? Tristan must've told him. "We don't want to hurt them. You know that, right?"

"I do, but this just got a thousand times more complicated." Kyle glanced over his shoulder. "Dylan's coming this way.

Thanks for hearing me out."

She nodded and left the cage. Dylan was waiting outside cage seven, smiling. "Alyssa! What are you doing here?"

"I work here. It's, uh, it's my dad's place." She cringed inside, wondering if that meant her one safe place with Tristan was about to be Dylan's new hangout, too. "I've worked here since I was old enough to load a pitching machine."

"Did you play?"

Holding in a sigh, she nodded. "Softball, from age four to thirteen. I quit when I was fourteen to focus on dancing."

"Yeah, you were one of the dancers in the musical. I remember." He nudged her slightly. "You looked great up there."

Considering *Faith* had been the star of *Oklahoma!* and Alyssa was only an extra, it seemed Dylan had been checking her out for some time now. "Thanks. Do you need anything? We have quite a crowd, and I should…"

"Yes, oh, right. I'll let you get back to work. It's great seeing you." He gave her a wave and went into his cage.

Alyssa sent two other guys into four and six, then turned to find Tristan outside cage five. "Hey."

"Hey." He kept his expression neutral but winked at her.

She almost laughed but swallowed it down. "This cage is broken. Sorry. The first three are open."

"They're all taken, actually." He gave her a very quick smile. "I talked up Swing Away to the guys once Dylan suggested we come here, and a lot more joined us."

Her jaw dropped slightly. "You talked up Swing Away?"

"I did." He still acted like a slight acquaintance, but she saw the message in his eyes. "Top Sports only has outside cages. Swing Away is much better."

Almost in answer, several pitching machines went off, followed by two or three *tings* and a couple of curses. "We certainly appreciate the business."

He nodded. "Is there any place I can wait until a cage becomes free? A closet maybe?"

Alyssa flushed red-hot. "We do have a few closets in the building."

"Hey," a voice called from behind her. "Quit bothering the lady and start hitting!"

The tone was good-natured, but Tristan flinched. "This cage is out of order, Dylan. I'm hanging around until you're done so I can practice."

Alyssa gave him a tiny nod. "We have a snack bar, if you want to wait there. I'll show you."

Dylan watched her lead Tristan away, forehead wrinkled, and Alyssa was very careful to keep five paces between them.

When they rounded the corner, Alyssa motioned Tristan to the far side of the snack bar, out of sight of the cages. "What happened?"

"We were rained out, and Dylan started talking about coming here. I had no idea he knew about Swing Away." Tristan ran a hand through his hair, and Alyssa ached to smooth it down for him. "Look, I hate acting like I hardly know you, but I don't know what else to do."

"There isn't anything else we can do." She patted him on the arm. "I understand. I do. I can make it to Saturday if you can."

"About that…"

Alyssa stiffened. Was he going to draw this out? Was he embarrassed of her? "What about that?"

He gave her a pleading look. "Kyle knows about us. He… I told him. I'm sorry, but it slipped out. He's going to tell Faith, because she was trying to set me up with Lauren."

Oh, that's all. "I know—Kyle mentioned it."

He frowned. "You aren't mad?"

"No." She laughed. "I was worried you were going to keep me secret because you were embarrassed or something."

He winced. "No, not at all. Do you know Faith well? Can she keep a secret?"

"Oh, yeah." Alyssa laughed again, relieved. "She's great. Unless you're her ex-boyfriend."

Tristan laughed now, low in his throat. "That's the truth. Okay, I'm going to go back out there and razz some of the guys, like I'm trying to shoo them out of the cage so I can have a turn. You do…whatever you do when you have a crowd of obnoxious ballplayers taking over the place."

He glanced over her shoulder, then planted a quick kiss against her temple. She turned to watch him go and, a minute later, heard, "Okay, asshats, quit hogging the cages! I've been waiting around long enough!"

Alyssa hid a smile behind her hand and went back to work. Dad was at the front counter, selling another set of tokens to a kid who looked like a freshman. He nodded to her. "Chickadee, can you go see if the conveyor is moving balls back to the machines well?"

Right back to cages seven and eight… Dang it. "Sure."

"Chickadee?" the freshman repeated. "That's not her name, right?"

Dad's roar of laughter followed her down the line. It was great to see him this pepped up but not necessarily at her expense. Rolling her eyes, she made her way past cage eight, stopping a second to watch Kyle smash a ball all the way to the far net.

Dylan caught her looking and swung for the fences on the next pitch. He caught the edge of the ball and hit a little blooper, maybe a single if the second baseman wasn't a fast fielder. He gave her a sheepish smile. So much for trying to outdo Kyle Sawyer at the plate.

Alyssa flipped the control box for the conveyor open. All the lights were green, and no one seemed to be waiting on balls, but she took her time looking anyway. How long were they planning to stay?

She stared into the box as long as she could without looking like she was stalling and hurried down the walkway, like she had somewhere to be, but no such luck. Dylan called, "Hey, Alyssa? I think I have a problem with my pitching machine."

Of all the flipping luck. "On my way."

He opened the cage door and stepped aside to let her in, standing *just* close enough that her arm had to brush his in order to make it inside. Alyssa clenched her jaw. He was a nice guy and a good pitcher. She had to keep that in mind. "What's the trouble?"

"I'm not sure. It stopped working."

She went to look at the machine, fearing the worst—that they'd be down *three* cages instead of two—and sighed. "You're out of credits. You need to put a token in."

When she turned, Dylan was right behind her. "I know. I wanted a second to talk to you without everyone noticing."

Alyssa crossed her arms over her chest. "Okay."

"Look, I promised I wouldn't pressure you for an answer, and I won't, but I hope you consider going out with me. I've been thinking about you, and it's crazy that…here you are. Almost like it was fate or something." He flashed her a cute smile, one that probably worked on 99 percent of girls. "Can I text you Saturday, after the game?"

She couldn't see Tristan, but she saw Kyle glance over his shoulder and shake his head slightly. Those two were so protective of their pitcher it was almost funny. And it would've been, if she weren't caught in the middle. Reluctantly, she said, "Sure, you can text me."

"Great! I guess you're into baseball, working at a batting cage."

How do I get out of here? "Yes, and I was, uh, I was a pitcher."

"Really? We'll have to talk shop sometime." He flushed. "I mean, we don't have to—I don't force girls to endure baseball stories on dates."

Alyssa felt so bad. This guy really was sweet, but her attention belonged to someone else. "I... It's okay, really. Look, I need to get back to work. You guys are keeping us busy today."

"Oh, right!" He smiled. "Thanks for stopping by."

She let herself out of the cage, and Kyle caught her eye. He made a face and went back to work.

Alyssa shook her head and did the same.

Chapter Twenty

TRISTAN

Tristan slowly fed his last token into the pitching machine in cage two. He'd seen Alyssa bustling back and forth—and he'd seen her go into Dylan's cage. Were the rest of these guys ever going to leave? The rain hadn't abated one bit, but practice would've ended twenty minutes ago, and Swing Away closed in another hour. How long could he stand here and pretend to be busy?

How long was Dylan going to do the same thing?

Kyle ambled down the walkway, stopping outside Tristan's cage. "How's it going?"

Tristan paused his game. "It" probably meant his batting practice, and he shook his head. "Zen's playing hide-and-seek so far."

"A lot on your mind, huh?" Kyle gave him a knowing look. "Come to practice early tomorrow. We should talk."

Tristan nodded and went back to his game. First pitch—whiff. Second pitch—whiff. Third pitch—whiff. Fourth pitch—

whiff.

Tristan ground his teeth and paused the machine. He was so worried about Dylan pitching against Allen, he was making his own problems worse. It was his own fault, for sure, but that didn't make it any easier.

"Hey." Alyssa appeared at the cage door. "Slow down."

She gave him a quick smile, then walked back to the front counter. Slow down. That was a good motto for just about everything right now. Taking a deep breath, Tristan restarted the machine. When the next pitch came, he hesitated a half second before swinging.

Ting!

Ting!

Ting!

He glanced at the counter, and Alyssa gave him this "told you so" smile. He nodded.

Tristan went two out of three for the last few pitches, then stopped to stretch. How was it that two words from Alyssa could unwind everything inside him? He had it bad, that was for sure.

"Looking good." Dylan rapped on his cage door. "Finished? We could go to dinner?"

"Um, you know what? I might stay and hit another round. Mom said something about pizza tonight, so I think I'm safe to go home."

Dylan frowned and glanced at Alyssa. "I'll stay with you."

"No, it's fine." Tristan forced a sheepish expression. "I'm tired of showing my slump off to you guys. I'd like to hit alone for a while."

Dylan's frown deepened. "You were looking pretty good just now. Sure you want to keep hitting? You shouldn't overdo it."

Tristan shrugged, willing his friend to leave. "I'll be fine. See you tomorrow?"

"Yeah. See you tomorrow." Dylan glanced at him over his shoulder before stopping to chat with Alyssa.

Tristan pretended to stretch until Dylan was safely outside, then he packed his stuff and walked up front. "I thought they'd never go."

"Me, too." She gave him a tired smile. "It's late, but maybe we could grab dinner? Unless you need to run."

He leaned on the counter, drawing close. "I don't have anywhere else to be."

He gave her a light kiss, and she sighed softly. "I was hoping you'd say that." She turned toward the office behind the desk. "Dad, crisis averted, and all the guys are gone. Can I head out?"

"Sure," came a muffled reply. "See you at home later."

Alyssa grabbed her purse from under the counter and came around to take Tristan's hand. "So where should we—"

The bell above the door jingled, and Dylan swept in. "I forgot my bag."

He stopped as soon as he saw them, hand in hand. Tristan's gut clenched at the confusion and hurt on Dylan's face. "Man, look," he started. "I wanted to tell you, but…"

"But you didn't." Dylan's expression hardened. "Alyssa, you could've told me you were seeing someone."

"Hey, you're mad at me, okay?" Tristan stepped in front of Alyssa. "In all fairness, she turned you down, just like you thought. She let you down easy. I'm the one you should be pissed with."

"You could've told me. I would've understood." Dylan shook his head, and his face was flushed. "Fuck it, I'm out."

He turned and stomped out into the rain, leaving whatever he'd forgotten behind—if he'd left anything at all. Maybe it had been an excuse to come back inside. Tristan rubbed a hand over his face. "You okay?"

No answer.

Tristan turned to find Alyssa standing absolutely still, tears on her cheeks. "I'm sorry. He's your friend, and now…"

"Now it's my mess, okay? I'm the one who decided to keep it from him." And it would be Tristan's fault if the team lost on Friday—whether it was Dylan's pitching or his own lack of hitting. He put his arms around her. "It's not your fault."

She shook her head, and her phone pinged in her bag. "Shit, I knew it wouldn't take long, but that was fast." She pulled out her phone, looked at it, and squeezed her eyes shut. "I was right. Dylan already texted Lauren. She knows, too."

"God." Tristan rested his chin on her head. "What do you want to do?"

"I need to go see her." Alyssa pulled away and swiped at her cheeks. "Look, there's a lot going on. Maybe…maybe we should back off for a while. Until this blows over."

It was such a reasonable thing to say, and Alyssa was nothing if not a reasonable girl. Still, it hurt. "You mean you don't want to see me anymore?"

"Not forever." She swallowed hard, and he could tell she was close to breaking down again. "Just…until the playoffs are over. Or until we can help them understand."

Knowing what little he did about Lauren, he didn't see her understanding *ever*. Dylan might come around, but he was going to make Tristan pay for it for a while. Tristan pushed down the ache pounding in his chest, hating what he had to say. "If that's what you want."

"It's not, but it's what's right." She gave him a quick, tight hug, then released him. "Thanks for bringing the guys here."

He started to say it was Dylan's idea first but stopped. Selfish or not, he wanted credit for the one good thing that happened today. "You're welcome."

Tristan squeezed Alyssa's hand, then hauled his bag onto his shoulder and stepped out into the rain.

"What's wrong, son?" Dad stared at the uneaten piece of pizza on Tristan's plate. "You usually mow this stuff down."

"It's nothing." He picked at the pizza crust. How had everything gotten so fucked up in the space of five minutes?

No, he was lying to himself—in the space of four days. He was such an idiot. If he'd only explained things to Dylan. It wasn't like he'd known Alyssa was the girl Dylan liked, not at first. But when he figured it out, what did he do? He'd hidden it from everyone. And now he was alone—no Dylan, no Alyssa.

"I don't think it's nothing," Mom said. "Are you getting sick?"

Tristan shook his head. Anything to keep the thermometer out of his mouth. "I'm good. Just…tired."

His parents exchanged a look. Even if they didn't understand baseball, they understood *him* pretty well. Mom forced a smile. "Maybe you should get some rest, then? Big game this week, right?"

He nodded, feeling dull. "That's a good idea. I'm going to bed."

He left them, sure they were watching every step he took until he disappeared from their sight. When he was safely upstairs, locked away in his room, he hazarded a glance at his phone.

Nothing from Dylan, nothing from Alyssa.

There was a text from Kyle. *Dude, you okay?*

Wondering how far the news had spread, Tristan texted:

Not even a little. My own fault, tho.

Kyle didn't answer right away, which was proof enough. Tristan pulled off the clean T-shirt he'd worn to dinner and slid into bed. The rain hadn't let up for a minute, and an occasional thunderclap rumbled in the distance. Good weather for a crap mood.

His phone buzzed—Kyle again. *Don't beat yourself up. Things will be better tmo.*

Tristan hoped so, but as for believing it...he wasn't quite there yet.

Chapter Twenty-One

ALYSSA

"I can't believe you'd do that behind my back!" Lauren was pacing the floor of her bedroom, her pretty features twisted with anger. "You totally stole my guy!"

Faith rolled her eyes. "No, she didn't, Laur."

"Yes, she did!" Lauren glared at Alyssa. "You knew. You *knew* I liked him. Why would you do this to me?"

Alyssa stared at the quilt on Lauren's bed. The fact that she hadn't known wouldn't make a difference now. "I didn't mean to hurt you."

"But you did." Lauren paused as a tear ran down her face. "God, did you two laugh at me? When I went up to Snap's?"

Alyssa jumped to her feet. "No! Not at all!"

"But the fake girlfriend was you, right?" Lauren wiped her tears away. "Aren't I just the little idiot? You usually help me with guys. I should've known you were sneaking around."

What could Alyssa say to that? She had been sneaking, but she was also starting to get angry. "You barely know him.

I spent hours with him over the last few days. We have a lot in common. I get why you can't be happy about it, but can you at least try to understand how good this is for me?"

Lauren huffed out a breath. "You lie then ask me to understand? What's wrong with you?"

Faith groaned. "Lauren, try to listen for a minute, would you? Alyssa has a connection with Tristan. Maybe you would have, too, but we can't know that. I know this hurts, but you'll find someone. I can say from experience that unexpected love is the best kind of all."

Lauren ignored her, crossing the room to stand in front of Alyssa. "How'd you do it? How'd you win him away from me?"

Rage bloomed, vicious and red, in Alyssa's chest. "What are you saying? That I'd have to stoop to dirty tricks because no guy in his right mind would pick me over you? That's what you're thinking, right?"

"That's… That's not what I'm…" Lauren's face turned bright red. "Don't you turn this around on me!"

Alyssa's stomach rolled over. No matter what Lauren said, what she thought was clear. "Oh, I forgot. It's always about you. I'm here to be your sidekick. You know what? I'm done." She turned to go, ignoring Lauren's sharp inhale. "By the way, I put Tristan aside today. Maybe we'll get back together, maybe we won't. But I cared enough about you not to throw it in your face. Too bad you don't feel the same way about me."

Alyssa left the bedroom, shutting the door firmly behind her. Lauren's mother stood at the bottom of the stairs, her foot on the first step, like she was coming to break it up. "What's going on?"

"Nothing now." Alyssa trotted down the steps, past Mrs. Willet. "Nothing at all."

By the time she made it home, urging her Honda not to break down on the way, her parents had finished dinner. A plate was in the microwave, ready to be warmed up, but Alyssa wasn't hungry. She wandered toward the living room, thinking she'd sneak upstairs without talking to anyone, but her parents were sitting on the sofa, talking softly.

Grateful Buddy had run out the back door as soon as she opened it for him, Alyssa kept to the shadows and strained to listen.

"The inspector said he couldn't give me an extension, and the bank wouldn't extend me a loan," Dad was saying. "We're behind on the rent, and I'm not sure how I'm going to pay Alyssa for all her hard week the past week. Maybe I should just give up and close down early. The GM at Top Sports is calling me every other day. He is completely on board with my demands for Alyssa's job. At least we know *they* can pay her."

"We have four weeks, Grant. Let's give it a little more time before we decide," Mom said. "I'll find a way to pay Alyssa."

"Thanks, babe.

Alyssa squeezed her eyes shut, but tears crept through her eyelids anyway. The whole thing with Tristan and Lauren paled in comparison with the thought of Dad losing the business they both loved. Everything was a mess. But she could help, and she would.

She scrubbed her checks and pulled her checkbook out of her backpack. Her friends had laughed when they found out she had an actual checkbook, but practical was her middle name, and her parents both said there might be a time she needed a check.

Turned out, they were right.

She wrote Swing Away's name in the payee field and made the check out for $2,500…all she had.

Then she strode into the living room and held up the check. "Lauren and I aren't on speaking terms and probably won't be for a while. I don't want to go to ballet camp. I want you to take my money." She set it on the coffee table, ignoring the shocked look on her parents' faces. "And I'll work for free until we're out of the hole. I'm going upstairs to read more repair manuals for the pitching machines."

"We can't take this," Mom said, her mouth pulled down in a sad frown. "Honey, we can't."

"You can, and you will." She looked at her dad. "I'm now a silent partner. You'll pay me back; I know you will. Is that enough to repair the nets?"

Dad stared at the check, his shoulders slumped. "Just about. I can come up with the rest."

Finally. *Finally.* "Good. If I can fix the machines, and you paint the place, maybe we'll make it."

"But, 'Dee, it still might not be enough." Dad stood and put a hand on her arm. "What if I lose your money, too? I couldn't live with that."

Alyssa squared her shoulders. "I can."

Determination pushed her out of the living room and down the hall to her bedroom. Maybe school was screwed up. But she could fix this, and she would.

She pulled her ancient laptop onto the bed and pulled up the pitching machine company's troubleshooting site to take some notes on other things to try. Maybe there were some parts they needed to order.

Maybe if she concentrated on this enough, she wouldn't have to think about anything else.

An hour later, Alyssa dropped her pencil and stretched. She had three pages of notes, along with a list of parts and the name of a repair company in Dallas. Their service calls were ninety-nine dollars, but if she could talk her dad into having them come out…

Her phone buzzed. Out of habit, Alyssa looked at the screen. It wasn't Lauren, or even Tristan.

It was Faith.

Are you okay?

A: *No. But that was a long time coming. Sorry you had to see it.*

F: *I understand. Look, are you sure you shouldn't get back together with Tristan? I think he could be good for you. And vice versa.*

Alyssa stared at her phone, chest aching. No, she wasn't sure. All she knew is that she'd hurt four people this afternoon, and being with Tristan would ease her heart, but it wouldn't fix the situation they were in. Time and distance might help everyone involved…or it might not.

A: *Do you honestly think Laur would let it go if I did?*

There was a long pause before Faith responded.

No, probably not. I'm so sorry it turned out this way.

Alyssa's throat constricted, but she wasn't going to let herself cry. Not anymore. No matter how sweet and kind Faith was being about the whole thing.

A: *Me, too.*

Chapter Twenty-Two

TRISTAN

"Good luck," Tristan said to Dylan. They'd barely spoken off the field the last few days and were pointedly polite when they did.

"You, too." Dylan's voice was remote. Any other game day, Tristan would've chalked it up to nerves. He knew better this time.

Dylan had moved lunch tables and no longer waited for Tristan at their lockers in the morning. Tristan never saw Lauren, either, and on the rare occasion he caught sight of Alyssa, she gave him a sad smile but nothing more.

The week had been pure hell, and Tristan didn't see any way out of it. He'd apologized to Dylan, who'd shrugged it off like it was no big deal. Dylan's behavior told a different story, though, and by the time the game had rolled around, Tristan was thoroughly miserable.

"Shake it off, man." Kyle whacked his shoulder with his glove as they ran out of the dugout for the top of the first.

"Shake it off."

The home crowd was out in force, screaming and cheering as they took the field. Tristan rolled his neck and took his place in center field. Kyle jogged on to left field. It was time.

A horde of wasps awoke in Tristan's stomach. Every player was nervous at the start of a game. Healthy anxiety. But that's not what this was. Tristan squeezed his eyes shut, counted to five, then opened them again. No matter what he did, all he could see was Dylan's face at Swing Away, followed by Alyssa's when she'd let him go.

Pull it together. Dylan climbed onto the mound, and Tristan stood ready. The leadoff batter for Allen was no better than most, but the heart of their order was crazy good. Suttonville needed to go three and out.

The first pitch was high, and the batter watched it go by. Dylan stalked around the mound a bit, and Tristan heard the first baseman yelling encouragement. The next pitch was way inside.

Four pitches later, the Allen batter strolled to first base on a walk. The Suttonville catcher and first baseman went in to calm Dylan down, but all Tristan could do was watch and wait.

Dylan took the mound again. This time, he craned his neck around and stared at Tristan a moment before turning back and winding up.

And for the next six pitches, he threw nothing but strikes.

If there was one good thing about Dylan being pissed at him, it was that Tristan was providing a weird kind of motivation.

By the fourth batter, the best hitter at Allen, Dylan was in good form, throwing a mean curve and wicked changeup. On the fourth pitch, though, something happened. Dylan threw a fastball, but it lacked its usual punch, and the Allen batter managed a hit. The bail sailed up, up, up, straight for center field.

Tristan ran for the wall. In the corner of his eye, he could see Kyle running flat out, so Tristan waved him off. He had to catch this ball. Somehow he knew he could redeem everything if he just caught the ball.

The arc of the ball was dropping. It wasn't going to be a wall-snatcher, but a catch right on the dirt track. He could grab it, end the inning, and everything would be okay.

He reached for the ball, watching its trajectory. Almost there…almost…

The ball lipped the edge of his glove and rolled into the corner by the wall.

"Shit!" Tristan scrambled after it, scooped it up, and threw it to second base, but he was too late. The Allen runner was a jackrabbit and had turned his teammate's stand-up double into a run.

Dylan shot him a furious look, then caught a fresh ball from the catcher. The fifth hitter crushed the very first pitch toward left field. Kyle raced to the wall, jumped, and caught the damn ball over the edge of the fence. He saved the inning, but the damage was done, and it was Tristan's fault.

They jogged off the field. Dylan, who batted ninth, stalked over to the pitcher's area to pull a jacket sleeve over his left arm. Tristan could hear him cursing across the dugout.

"Enough," Coach snapped. "Murrell, what happened out there? You have to keep your eyes on it."

Tristan nodded. "Yes, sir. Sorry. I misjudged the distance."

But Coach had already turned away to praise Kyle's catch. Tristan, shoulders slumped, took the seat on the bench farthest away from Dylan. He hadn't missed a catch that easy in weeks. They probably scored the run on an error, so at least it wouldn't hurt Dylan's stats, but still.

There was a *ting!* and all the heads in the dugout peered out as their second baseman ran hard for first, beating the throw and ending up safe. Their catcher struck out, but the shortstop hit a little blooper to shallow right, and the runners advanced. It was Tristan's turn.

He took his place in the batter's box. *Slow down.* If he could get a solid hit, they could tie it up or take the lead. He breathed nice and slow. He could do this.

The first pitch, a blistering fastball, sailed under his bat on the first swing.

"Strike!" the umpire called.

The second pitch, another fastball, came flying at him, and Tristan managed to catch the corner, fouling it off behind first base.

"Strike!"

Tristan clenched his jaw. The pitcher wound up and threw a changeup.

Tristan swung for it and caught a piece of the ball. It went right at the second baseman, who caught it on the fly and tagged up. That was it.

"You hit into a double play?" Coach looked incredulous. "Where's your head, son?"

Tristan dropped his bat and gathered up his glove. "Sorry. I'll do better. Promise."

Dylan shot him a dirty look and trotted up the stairs. Kyle came after him, shaking his head. "Come on, we have work to do."

"I can't believe we won," Jackson was saying to anyone who'd listen. "In spite of Murrell."

Tristan's hands clenched into fists. The first inning had been bad, and so what if he'd struck out twice and flied out once? He still caught everything that came his way for the rest of the game, including the final out.

Kyle pointed a finger at Jackson. "You shut up. Otherwise,

next time you blow a lead, I'm going to be on your ass."

"Murrell! I need to see you in my office." Coach's voice cut through the chatter, and the locker room hushed.

There was only one reason Coach called you into his office.

Tristan threw his glove into his equipment bag and trudged to the door at the back of the locker room. Coach's office was cluttered with coffee cups, papers, and jersey samples. Tristan took the seat in front of the desk and waited for Coach to finish typing something on his laptop.

When he finally glanced up, he looked pained. "Murrell, I can't bench you. Not now. We have two more games to go — the semis and the championship. Tutton isn't ready to take over for you, and certainly not during the playoffs. But if you fall apart next week like you did tonight, I'm going to be forced to do something. We won by pure dumb luck, and I like to win due to skill and smart play. Understand?"

Tristan stared at his hands folded in his lap. Marks from his glove still marred his skin. "I understand. I've had a rough week. That's all."

"And your swing?" At Tristan's shocked look, Coach rolled his eyes. "I've been watching you struggle for weeks. You can't hide that stuff from me. Whatever's going on, make it right. Maybe that will cure the demon in your head. Now go home and get some sleep, will you?"

Tristan nodded and turned to go. "I'm sorry. Really."

"I know you are. Hang in there, okay?"

Tristan slipped out of Coach's office. Most of the guys had already gone, but Kyle was still there, waiting for him.

"Did he bench you?"

"No." Tristan sat heavily on the locker room bench. "But he might."

"Look, it's none of my business, but Dylan did just fine tonight." Kyle picked up his bag and stood. "So even if he's mad at you—it's not affecting his game."

"I guess not." Tristan stood, too. "But I'm a mess."

"You are." Kyle smiled at him. "And there's a solution. If you want to be with Alyssa, go for it. Stop worrying about what Dylan wants or feels, and start worrying about yourself. A good thing doesn't come around often. Take my word for it."

He headed for the locker room exit and waved over his shoulder. Tristan watched him go, wondering if it was all that simple.

And if it was, would Alyssa take him back?

Chapter Twenty-Three

When Alyssa came into work Saturday, she had to stop and stare at the bright white, brand-new netting stretched across the back of the cages. She'd done that, and it made everything look new. Good thing, because that was all she had going for her at the moment.

She'd hoped Lauren would come around, that something as simple as a guy wouldn't come between them, but she'd underestimated her friend's ability to hold a grudge.

Alyssa choked back a humorless laugh as she fiddled with the guts of cage five's pitching machine. Lauren's ability to hold a grudge was legendary. If she was being honest with herself, Alyssa had to admit that, before, she hadn't *cared*.

Other than a pair of middle school girls who had the look of select-team softball players, the building was quiet. Too quiet for a Saturday. Dad was in his office, probably staring at the pile of bills, willing them to shrink before his eyes.

Alyssa's chest heaved with rage. Rage with no outlet. She

didn't like saying it wasn't fair—what was?—but she thought they would've caught a break by now. *If we go under, I bought those new nets for nothing.*

She slammed her screwdriver into the pitching machine's side. Being selfish didn't help things. Action did, but she was fresh out of ideas.

Alyssa sat on the floor, leaning against the machine, and covered her face. What more could she do? Was there anything else? Could she swallow her pride and work at Top Sports? It seemed like she'd have to. She needed a job.

The bell at the front door dinged, and she forced herself up. "Coming!"

She rounded the corner…and there was Tristan. He had his bag slung over his shoulder and was wearing one of those tight, sleeveless Under Armor shirts. Miles of tan, strong arms were on display, but she couldn't bring herself to ogle them.

With Lauren on a rampage, and Dylan hurt, she needed to stay away. *What was that about things not being fair?*

"I, um, I need the practice." He flushed and stared at the floor. "I had some issues last night."

She nodded wearily. "My dad told me—he went to the game. Cage eight is open if you want it."

His expression turned hopeful. "Any chance you could give me some pointers?"

Alyssa held up her screwdriver. "I'm still working on the pitching machine in five."

"Right." The disappointment on his face made her bones ache. "If you change your mind, you know where I'll be."

He trudged down the lane and opened the cage door.

Alyssa stayed at the counter and waited. A few minutes later, the pitching machine whirred and clicked. No *ting!* followed.

No. Let him work it out. Alyssa polished the countertop with a rag she kept on a shelf below the register. *He doesn't need you. You don't need him.*

Her heart ached… It knew she was lying to herself, and it made sure to let her know. She wiped the counter down with more vigor, scrubbing at a years-old coffee stain. The thing was never coming up, but she was going to scrub it until the counter cracked if that was what it took.

No matter how hard she worked, her ear automatically registered everything going on in cage eight. Too many years spent listening to batters was an impossible habit to break. The machine threw another ball. No hit. And another. And another.

This time the miss was followed by a "goddamn it!" The woman waiting on the two softball girls lowered her magazine and frowned. She shot Alyssa a look.

Alyssa bit the inside of her cheek. Nothing for it… She had to go down there. She nodded at the woman. "I'll tell him to keep it down."

She dropped her rag back on the shelf, steeled herself, and walked down to Tristan's cage. The machine was on pause, and he was sitting on the bench with his head bowed and his hands dug into his hair. His bat lay tossed away in the far corner.

Alyssa blinked back stinging tears. This guy was wrecked…and she had a nasty feeling it was partly her fault. Gathering up her courage, she cleared her throat.

Tristan's head popped up. His face was a picture of pure misery. "What?"

If he'd snapped at her like that earlier, she would've jerked back and glared at him. Today, she opened the cage door and gave his shoulder a push to nudge him over on the bench. To her surprise, he moved without arguing.

The bench was narrow enough that they had to sit shoulder to shoulder, and the warmth of his skin made her regret all her decisions the last several days. "You're overthinking it,

Murrell. Your head space is full of ugly, and it's tearing you apart, taking your batting skills with it."

"Kind of hard to be all unicorns and daisies when my best friend has written me off and the girl I like pushed me away." He looked at her, and his eyes seared her down to her soul. "Dylan might get over it, he might not. But, Alyssa, I want to give us a try anyway."

She let herself lean against Tristan's side. In a way, he was right. If everything else was going to hell, why shouldn't she see what could happen with him? Lauren probably *wouldn't* get over it, but she was going to be pissy whether Alyssa dated Tristan or not, now that the cat was out of the bag.

"Why?" she asked. "Why me?"

He laughed softly. "Are you serious?"

"Yeah." She shifted to face him. "Why am I enough to possibly lose your best friend?"

His eyes widened. "You really don't know, do you?"

She shrugged. "You like curly hair and curves. And I know about baseball. But that's not really enough."

"You're funny and determined. You put me in my place." He grinned, slow, and she flushed. "And, like I said, I like a girl who knows how to fix things. Batters, pitching machines, whatever else. You aren't one of those 'flirty one minute, sulky the next' kind of girls. You're the real deal."

Alyssa stared down at her hands. She'd always found them too…capable. Not delicate enough. But what if capable was a good thing? What if practical wasn't a curse? "Oh."

He tucked a stray strand of hair behind her ear. "Now, you. Why am I enough to write off Lauren?"

Alyssa smiled up at him. "Well, you've met her."

Tristan laughed. "That I did. What else?"

"I don't know. I've known a lot of ballplayers. Most of them are players off the field, too. Looking for a quick hit, an easy score. You go deeper. You look at things on a different level." She stared into his eyes. They were such a warm brown that she felt like she could fall into them and drift. "And you like girls who wield screwdrivers. Some guys are threatened by that. My last boyfriend, for example. I wasn't 'girly' enough for him. Too much time in running shorts and not enough time in skirts."

Tristan shook his head. "He was an idiot."

"I don't know. I don't really fit the mold, you know?" Still, her heart swelled a little to hear that a guy could like her for *her*. "And…I'd like to give us a try, too."

"Good." His face moved closer to hers. "I needed to hear that."

Then he was kissing her, and it felt so right. The way his lips moved softly against hers, not demanding anything. She scooted a little closer and slipped an arm around his waist, hoping her dad wasn't lurking nearby. Tristan smiled against her mouth and toyed with her hair. It was so sweet she wanted to do this all afternoon.

"Jesus, Murrell. Get a room." A guy honked out the most annoying laugh Alyssa had ever had the misfortune of hearing. "There's no kissing in baseball, man."

Alyssa jumped—the voice had come from the next cage over. Usually cage seven's door creaked, but she hadn't heard a thing. She hadn't even heard the bell over the front door ding.

Tristan was bad for her concentration.

He pressed his forehead against Alyssa's. "Excuse me while I go punch Jackson."

She pulled away and winked at him. "You like strong girls? Watch this."

She got up and leaned against the fence between the two cages. "Tell you what. You can talk trash all you want, so long as you get a hit before I do."

Jackson, a stocky kid with the look of a pampered pitcher,

rolled his eyes. "You're on."

She picked up Tristan's bat and rolled her shoulders. "You're up, sunshine," she told Jackson.

"You're letting me go first? Bad idea, sweetheart."

"Did you just call her 'sweetheart,' asshole?" Tristan barked.

Jackson laughed and started his machine. *Whir*, *click*, pitch—a slider. Jackson swung, caught the edge of it, and smirked. "I win, *sweetheart*."

"I said a hit, not a foul ball. That's a strike." Alyssa smirked right back. "At least get the rules right before you talk crap."

She punched the pitch button on her machine. A moment later a ball flew out—fastball, low. Alyssa swung with her whole body.

Ting!

The ball sailed out into the middle pit. Alyssa paused the machine and put a hand on her hip. "From now on, you use your manners in my house, got it?"

Jackson stared at her. "What the hell was that?"

Tristan was laughing so hard he almost fell over on the bench. "I could've warned you, but why? You had it coming."

Jackson grumbled something under his breath and turned his machine back on.

Alyssa handed the bat to Tristan. "I really do need to get back to work, but I want to watch you take a swing first."

Tristan drew a deep breath and nodded. "Here goes nothing."

"Good head space. Slow down." She smiled encouragingly and backed out of the cage. Tristan started the machine, and it pitched him an off-speed changeup. He swung, and immediately Alyssa could see a difference. His movement was looser, more confident. He cracked the ball right off the sweet spot of his bat, and it flew out to the middle pit and landed almost next to hers.

He grinned over his shoulder. "Coach needs to hire you as the batting assistant. I'm serious."

"Nah, I'd curse out his players and get fired." She grinned back. "Keep after it. I'm going to wrestle with a pitching machine for a while."

"Wanna wrestle with a pitcher instead?" Jackson called. "I'm available."

Alyssa turned a glare on him. "No, thank you. I have too much self-respect."

She left Tristan howling with laughter and stalked up front to grab her tool kit. What was with diva pitchers not thinking girls knew their own minds? First Dylan refused to believe she was turning him down, and now Jackson acted like an asshat—in front of a guy she'd just kissed.

She opened the door to cage five and pulled the cover off the pitching machine. It was hard to focus on the task, because her thoughts kept wandering back to Tristan, especially since the sound of a bat hitting a baseball came regularly from cage eight. He was doing better—was she his good luck charm? She'd gladly claim that title if it made him happy. It made her happy, too.

She lost track of time, and before long, a shadow fell over her and the obstinate pitching machine. Alyssa turned, and Tristan was smiling down at her. "Is it behaving yet?"

"No." She pushed herself up and dusted off her jeans. "I think it's probably hopeless. These machines are almost as old as I am. We need new ones, which sucks, because we can't afford new ones."

Tristan wound an arm around her waist. "I hate that. This is a nice place. It's *real*. I wish I could help."

"Being sweet always helps." She shoved a few strands of hair over her shoulder. "Thank you."

He pulled her into a full hug, and she leaned in, enjoying the feel of his body against hers. Why couldn't other things be as simple as a good hug from a cute guy?

"I better go. My mom told me if my room wasn't clean by sundown I'd lose my car for a week." He grimaced. "It's going to take that long to clean it.

Alyssa laughed. "Good luck with that. See you tomorrow?"

He shook his head. "I wish, but my family is having a brunch thing. My brother's coming home from college today, and we're celebrating by avoiding my mom's cooking. Monday?"

She smiled, feeling shy. "Monday."

He left, whistling, and she skipped to the front desk. A new lightness had settled in her soul. Something with Tristan might work out after all. He knew how to make her feel like she was special, and it seemed like she could do the same for him. This could even be the real deal, in the long run. Time would tell, but she had a good feeling.

Jackson came by the front desk, strutting like a peacock. "You have him all tied up, huh?"

Alyssa cocked her head, meeting his stare head-on. "So?"

"Guess he took my advice." Jackson headed for the door. "He found a slumpbuster."

Alyssa felt the blood drain from her face even as a cold, hard rage built in her chest. "What did you say?"

"Nothing."

"Bullshit." She came around the counter, glaring a hole in his forehead. "I've been around baseball and baseball players my entire life, and I know what a slumpbuster is."

"Good." Jackson winked at her. "Then I won't have to explain it. I told him he needed to find himself one last week, and here you are. He did good."

He walked out the door, leaving her spluttering curses at his back.

Once the anger faded, though, tears filled her eyes.

Was Jackson just being a nasty piece of work, or could it be true? Tristan's arrival had been perfect—too perfect. What if showing up at Swing Away was a calculated move?

What if he was using her, the homeliest girl he could find, to break his slump?

If he was, how lucky could one guy be? He'd found not only the perfect slumpbuster, but a girl who knew the sport well enough to fix technical issues, too.

Her stomach roiled. What if she'd not only been set up but had risked losing her best friend on a bad bet?

Every hurt from the last week came crashing down on her at once, and Alyssa sank down behind the counter and cried.

Chapter Twenty-Four

"How's my favorite little brother?" Keller rubbed Tristan's head, grinning.

"Younger, not little. You had to stand on tiptoe to mess up my hair." Tristan patted his hair back into place. "I'm fine. How's school?"

"It's school." Keller shrugged. "Engineering, math, fifteenth-century British lit for fun."

"You're reading old English for fun? Way to make me look like a slacker, butthead." Tristan felt pride swell in his chest anyway. His brother was a genius, and how many people could say that? "It's good to have you home."

"Yeah. I can't wait to watch you play Friday." Keller threw a furtive glance at their parents, who were already at their favorite table in the country club's restaurant. "Can Mom tell the difference between balls and strikes, yet?"

Tristan snorted. "No. And Dad's still baffled by double plays. How can two smart people have that much trouble with a pretty simple sport? Football has about a thousand more rules than baseball."

"Don't worry about it." Keller led him toward the table. "I'll cheer enough for both of them. And maybe elbow them a little when you do something spectacular."

Only if my hitting keeps improving. He turned his head to hide a smile. Alyssa was definitely his secret weapon on Friday. The game was in San Antonio, so she probably couldn't come, but he'd make sure to steal a kiss or two Thursday night.

"What's the grin for?" Keller was watching with narrowed—amused—eyes. "Ah, who is she?"

"I'm that easy to read, huh?" Tristan paused beside the buffet, the smell of bacon calling to him like a siren song. His stomach rumbled. "Her name's Alyssa. That's all you get before I'm fed."

After filling plates, they joined their parents. Tristan concentrated on eating, especially when the conversation turned to thermodynamics. The rest of his family chatted easily about stuff that made his brain hurt. Sure, they loved him, but sometimes he felt he was on a different planet than the rest of them.

"Hey," Keller shot him a look. "How about this kid. The team is in the semis. That's hard-core, right?"

"Um...yes?" Mom's forehead wrinkled. "Is hard-core good?"

Dad chuckled. "It's rad."

Tristan groaned and laid his head on the table. "Please, make them stop."

"No, really, we should let them go on." Keller was snickering. "I want to see how long until Dad dredges up 'gnarly.'"

"Hey, don't mock our generation's teenage exclamations," Dad said. "You people say things like 'yasss queen.' I have no idea who you're talking about. Queen Elizabeth?"

"Noooo," Tristan moaned. "This has gone too far. Stop

talking. Please, for the love of God."

"You know we love you, honey." Mom shook his arm, smiling when he looked up at her. "And we are proud of the baseball. You do well."

Wow…what praise. Not great, just well. "Thanks Mom."

"Now, about that girl." Keller waggled his eyebrows. "What's the story there?"

"Girl?" Mom asked, perking up. "There's a girl? I thought we were still in the post-Raina grief cycle."

"Mom, I know you did a psych rotation in med school, but there was no grief cycle." Not entirely true, but he was definitely over it—it'd been almost a year already. "And yes, there's a girl. She's, uh, like me. She's into baseball, but she's also a dancer."

"Ballet?" Mom's eyes were shining now. "Please tell me it's ballet."

"It's ballet." Tristan rolled his eyes. What, did she think he was going to tell her Alyssa was into exotic dancing? "She's trying out for the Dallas Ballet Conservatory camp in the summer."

"How wonderful. A cultured young lady. I bet she knows all about classical music, too."

Tristan's heart sank a little. Hearing Alyssa was like him hadn't interested Mom—the parts that were like *her* did. "Maybe. I guess. I don't know."

"Is she a junior? Does she know where she'll go to university?" Dad asked.

"I…I don't know, exactly." Tristan swallowed hard. He really didn't know as much about Alyssa as he should. They spent a lot of their time together working on his hitting issues. Well, and worrying about Swing Away. For some reason, not knowing more bothered him. He wanted to know *her*. There were a thousand questions he wanted to ask her now, from her favorite ice cream flavor to whether or not she planned to go to college in-state or across the country. "I'll ask her when I see her again."

That satisfied Dad, but Mom was like a hound with a scent. "What does she look like? Do you have a picture? If you're still together at homecoming, can I make her a mum? Oh, where does she live? Do you know her mother's name?"

"Mom, go easy on him." Keller pointed a piece of bacon Tristan. "He looks like he's going to drown under all the questions. Let him get to know the girl before you do, okay?"

"Oh, of course." Mom's cheeks turned a light pink. "I'm sorry, honey."

"It's okay." Tristan gave her a wry smile. "Give me another month or two, and I'll not only answer all your questions, I'll bring her over to meet you."

Mom nodded, satisfied. Or so he thought until she said, "Keller, what about you? Any young ladies we need to chat about?"

Keller held up a hand and called, "Check, please."

Tristan sat cross-legged on his bed, staring at his phone. After he'd finished his homework, he'd texted Alyssa. An hour later, she hadn't responded. Maybe it was nothing—maybe she was at work and couldn't get to her phone.

Still, he couldn't shake the feeling that something was wrong. He had no idea why, but sometimes gut feelings were right even without any evidence.

For a while, he thought maybe he was paranoid, but when he hadn't heard from her by Monday morning, doubts began to crowd out any reason he could muster up. He looked for her in the halls on his way to his locker and struck out. She had to be here somewhere. What was going on?

Dylan was leaning against his locker when Tristan walked

up. Stealing himself for the silent treatment, Tristan forced a friendly smile. "Hey. How was your weekend?"

"Okay." Dylan stared at the tile floor. "Look, I was kind of a bastard last week. I had some time to think about everything, and I get why you didn't tell me at first."

Shock coursed through Tristan. "Seriously? You're…okay?"

Dylan shrugged, but he was smiling a little, too. "Yeah, man, I am. I'm not in a good place for a girlfriend anyway. I want to make the minors in a year, and I need to focus on my game. My 'no girls' rule was for a good reason, and I'm sticking to it."

Tristan elbowed him in the ribs. "There's always Lauren."

Dylan's expression said it all. "Honestly, she's scary. I get the feeling she doesn't like it if she doesn't get her way. Not what I'm looking for, even if the package is nice." He jerked his chin at Tristan. "How about you and Alyssa? What's going on there?"

"I'm not sure… Well, I am, but…" He opened his locker and pulled out his binder for first period. "I like her, a lot. She's cool, and pretty, *and* a batting coach. I'll tell you right now, she's how I'm busting my slump."

"For real?" Dylan laughed. "I wondered how you got it back all of a sudden."

"For real." Tristan laughed, too. "She diagnosed my swing in, like, two tries. Just thinking about her smile is enough to slow me down so I can connect with a pitch."

"That's great. I really mean that." Dylan hoisted his backpack onto his shoulder. "Look, I better run. See you at lunch."

Tristan waved at his friend, then took one more look down the hall. He could've sworn he saw Alyssa's back, but by the time he waded through the students crowding the hall, she was gone.

His good mood fizzled. What was going on?

Chapter Twenty-Five

Monday was *not* going well. Tristan had texted her over and over Sunday, like nothing was wrong. She knew she needed to confront him, but she didn't have the energy and decided to deal with it at school. Except she'd woken up late, then the Honda took four tries to start, and now...

Now she was standing just around the corner from Tristan and Dylan. It looked like they'd made up, which was good, but what they were saying *wasn't*.

"I'll tell you right now, she's how I'm busting my slump," Tristan said.

"For real?" Dylan laughed. "I wondered how you got it back all of a sudden."

"For real." Tristan laughed, too.

Bile rose in Alyssa's throat as she backed away. Oh, God—it was true. Jackson hadn't been trolling her. Tristan had been using her all along.

She cupped a hand over her mouth and shoved her way

through the students in the hall. Ducking into the bathroom, she headed straight for a stall. Once safely inside, she leaned against the door and let out a shaking breath.

She'd been so wrong about him. Even with her doubts on Saturday after Jackson had razzed her, she hadn't believed it, not really. She'd needed time to cool off, sure, but part of her had held out hope that this was the real thing after all. Instead, she was nothing but the plain Jane a baseball player charmed to improve his stats.

A tear slid down her cheek. Maybe fate had simply decided her life should suck for a while. Or maybe she was just a stupid girl who saw what she wanted to see.

"'Lys? Is that you?" Lauren knocked on the stall door. "I'd know those royal-blue Converse anywhere. Are you okay?"

Alyssa wiped her running nose. "Are you talking to me?"

"Of course I am." Her voice was so kind Alyssa started to cry again. "I was a bitch, and you're right. If you could've trusted me not to overreact about Tristan, you would've told me."

"You can have him," Alyssa choked out.

"What?" Lauren knocked again. "Let me in there."

"Ew," another girl said. "Sharing a stall?"

"Shut up," Lauren snapped. "Boy emergency here."

The girl snorted. "Whatever. I'm leaving, so you two do you."

The warning bell rang. They had seven minutes until first period.

"I'll be okay," Alyssa said. "Go on to class."

"I'm not leaving until you come out or let me in."

"Fine." Alyssa opened the door and went to the sink to splash water on her face. "So, I misjudged Tristan. I thought he was different, but turns out I'm his slumpbuster."

Lauren frowned. "I'm not following."

"A slumpbuster is a DUFF you nail to break a hitting slump. Baseball players go after plain girls and try to hook up with them. It's a superstition. Damned baseball players and their stupid rituals."

"That… Okay, I don't think that's true. He seems like a really nice guy." Lauren laughed sadly. "I poured it on thick last week, and he couldn't get away fast enough. This doesn't sound like him."

"I *heard* him talking about it with Dylan." Alyssa met Lauren's eyes in the mirror. "He said I was busting his slump. What else would that mean?"

"I don't know. But we're going to find out." Lauren put her hands on her hips. "Count on it."

Alyssa barely kept Lauren from marching over to Tristan and Dylan's table at lunch and demanding to know what was going on. She'd avoided Tristan all morning, and she'd flat out ignored Dylan's smile and wave.

Now both guys were staring in their direction, looking concerned. Dylan whispered something in Tristan's ear, and he shook his head before standing.

"Oh, he's coming this way." Lauren had a manic gleam in her eye. "Goody."

Alyssa threw her napkin down on her tray. "Don't. I'm too tired to deal with this. Life is bad enough."

"Wait… Is something else going on?" Lauren touched Alyssa's arm. "I know I haven't been listening, but I am now."

Alyssa stood. "I'll meet you at the studio after school and tell you about it, but right now, I need out of here. Can you take my tray?"

"Sure." Lauren watched her leave, her mouth turned down.

Alyssa burst through the back doors. Black clouds roiled on the western horizon, and she was glad. A good thunderstorm felt right for today.

"Are you okay?"

She closed her eyes. The clouds had kept her from seeing his shadow approach. Now she had nowhere to go. "No."

Tristan stepped up behind her, close enough that his chest brushed her back, and a little thrill ran down her spine. She cursed her reaction—how could you be so disgusted with someone but still want them, too? It wasn't right.

"Are you going to tell me what I did?" he asked, his breath tickling the back of her neck. "Because whatever it is…I want to fix it."

"So you can bust your slump?" Her tone was bitter. "Because you found the perfect candidate to help with that?"

"Bust my slump? What are you talking about?"

She spun around so that they were face-to-face. Another inch closer, and they'd be kissing. Not that she'd ever be doing that again. "Jackson told me how you took his advice and found yourself the perfect slumpbuster. And how wonderful for you—not only do you find a perfectly plain girl, but you found one who knows something about baseball. Well, I'm not standing for it. I have some self-respect, you asshole."

She turned to walk away, but Tristan caught her arm. "Jackson called you my slumpbuster? I'm going to kick his ass from here to Sunday."

She jerked her arm out of his grasp. "Don't act like you knew nothing about this. I heard you talking to Dylan this morning. 'I'll tell you right now, she's how I'm busting my slump.' You can't blame Jackson for something *you* said."

"Alyssa, you misunderstood." His eyes were panicked. "This isn't like that. I *swear* that to you."

"Leave her alone." Lauren walked up and stood between them. "You don't deserve her."

Alyssa choked back a sob. It'd been a long time since her best friend had come to her rescue, and she hadn't realized how much it would mean.

Tristan wouldn't look at Lauren—he kept staring at Alyssa. "Please, just listen. You've got this all wrong."

"Go." Lauren gave Alyssa a little push. "I'll handle this."

Alyssa didn't need any other encouragement—she turned and ran.

Chapter Twenty-Six

TRISTAN

"Lauren, I do *not* think of Alyssa that way. My hand to God." Tristan held up his right hand. "I'm crazy about her. What she heard this morning—I was praising her skills at diagnosing what was wrong with my swing. That, and just thinking about her settles me down when I'm at the plate. I *swear* that's all."

Lauren's expression was blank. "Then why would she believe otherwise?"

"Because there's an asshole pitcher on my team. She embarrassed him Saturday—and rightfully so—and I guess that was his way of getting back at her." And when Tristan saw Jackson again, there was going to be a reckoning of biblical proportions. "I don't know where she's getting the idea she's plain or homely—she's not. She's beautiful. She's..." He dragged in a long breath. "She's perfect."

Lauren's shoulders relaxed. They'd been up around her ears, but he could tell she was thawing out. "Swear on your mother."

"What?"

"Swear on your mother." Lauren crossed her arms. "Or on Babe Ruth. I don't care. I almost believe you, but I need some kind of grand statement here."

His mouth worked. Was she serious? He wasn't going to take any chances. "I swear on Babe Ruth, the '98 Yankees, and Nolan Ryan's punch to Ventura's head. With the baseball gods as my witness."

She nodded. "Okay. I'll work on her. Do me a favor—give her space. She needs some time to calm down. Something else is eating her, but I don't know what."

"I do." He ran a hand across his forehead—he'd broken out in a cold sweat. "Swing Away's in trouble. She's been trying to help her dad save it, but it's not working."

Lauren froze. "Her dad's business is in trouble? She never told me."

Tristan held in a cringe. "It kind of came up when I was there practicing. It slipped out, I think. She's really upset."

"She would be." Lauren glanced in the direction Alyssa had run. "I need to go find her. I'll let you know when the coast is clear. It might not be for a few days, but you can trust me."

After that dinner at Snap's, Tristan was surprised to realize he *did* trust her. "I know."

"And about my flirting the other night…" She blushed and looked down at her shoes. "I'm sorry for putting you on the spot like that."

"It's fine, really." He laughed a little. "Work a miracle here, and I'll forget it ever happened."

"Deal. I better go. I'll text you when I know something." Lauren paused. "While you're waiting, maybe you can come up with something to save Swing Away. *That* would get her attention."

She turned and left him standing on the patio. Save Swing

Away. How on earth could he do that? A bake sale?

Shaking his head, Tristan went back inside.

"You said *what?*" Dylan's face was red, and he was jabbing a finger into Jackson's chest. "What the hell is wrong with you?"

Tristan sat on the bench, smirking in satisfaction. Turned out the pitching captain wanted to handle Jackson's stunt with Alyssa. Kyle stood behind Dylan, arms crossed, adding some weight to the chewing out.

Jackson's eyes darted over to Tristan. "It was just a joke. What's the big deal?"

Tristan stood, slowly, and took a step in his direction. "You made her feel bad. And you don't get to make my girl feel bad without consequences."

"Coach says no fighting." Jackson wore a belligerent expression.

"That's right," Kyle said, his words clipped and dangerous. "But I don't like bullies...never have. The season's almost over, and I graduate soon. I don't have much to lose. *And* I'm patient."

Jackson glared at Tristan. "You gonna let him fight your battle?"

He shrugged. "Sawyer seems to be doing a pretty good job of it. Still, if you apologize to Alyssa *and* tell her you were lying, you'll dig yourself out of this hole. Otherwise, I can't make any guarantees."

You could almost see the kid weighing his options. *Good cop, bad cop isn't just for movies, is it?* Tristan tapped his wrist. "Clock's ticking."

"Fine, I'll find her tomorrow and tell her I'm sorry."

Tristan nodded. "Good. Go hit the showers. The adults need to chat."

Jackson rolled his eyes and took off. Tristan waited until the door to the locker room closed. "You two notice I didn't hit a fucking thing today?"

"Hey, you've had a bad day. Don't freak out. You were doing better—one practice doesn't mean anything." Dylan chucked him on the shoulder with his glove. "By Friday, you'll have this sorted out with Alyssa, and we'll go win the championship."

Tristan wanted to believe it. He really did. But the dull ache behind his breastbone told him otherwise. "I hope so."

Kyle stood and stretched. "You know what I do when I'm messed up?"

"Um, we *all* know what you do to blow off steam," Dylan said, laughing.

"Not that." Kyle's ears turned pink. "I go for a long run. Clears the head." He picked up his equipment bag and headed for the locker room before saying, "Well, and the other thing, too."

"Running is the very last thing I want to do right now." Groaning, Tristan bent to put his bat away and zip up his bag. "I hurt everywhere."

"Go home, Tristan. Sleep. That's what you need." Dylan gave him a small shove to move him toward the locker room. "You'll figure this out. Stop worrying so much."

He nodded, but deep down, he wasn't sure he could.

Chapter Twenty-Seven

Alyssa sat on the smooth wooden floor in Madame Schuler's back studio, watching Lauren practice. Faith sat next to her, phone in hand.

"What did he say?" Alyssa asked.

"Oh, just that they got to the bottom of it." Faith's eyes sparkled. "Knowing Kyle, that means he stood over Jackson and glowered until he cried."

"So you're sure Jackson was making all this up?" Alyssa asked, trying to tamp down the hope threatening to burst free. She couldn't let herself be disappointed or hurt again. "Or is Tristan just a good liar?"

Lauren sighed and turned. "He likes you. A lot."

"And Jackson is a punk. Kyle told me so," Faith said. "Don't sell yourself short believing all that garbage."

Alyssa bowed her head to hide the tears filling her eyes. "Okay."

Lauren crossed the floor and sat next to Alyssa. Putting

an arm around her shoulders, she said, "You're exactly who he wants. He told me…" She laughed softly. "He said you're perfect."

"He did?" Alyssa sniffled. "No guy's ever said that about me before."

"None of those guys were Tristan Murrell. He swore on Nolan Ryan's punch to Ventura's head. I don't know exactly what that means, but it sounded important, so I bought it."

Alyssa burst into laughter, crying at the same time. "It's important."

"I thought so." Lauren shifted so she could lean against Alyssa's side. "Now, what's this about Swing Away? And why aren't you practicing with me?"

"He told you, then." Alyssa heaved a sigh and sat up straighter. "We're going under. We have less than two weeks to come up with enough money to fix the pitching machines, add a couple handicapped spaces in the parking lot, and stop a leak in the roof. We fixed the broken nets." She met Lauren's eyes. "I paid for them with my dance camp money."

Lauren's hand flew to her mouth. "Oh, 'Lys. Why didn't you tell me?"

"I'm upset." She closed her eyes… That wasn't quite right. "I'm ashamed. That we failed."

"You didn't fail. Neither did your dad." Faith scooted to her other side. "It's been rough out there since the recession. Plus, stupid Top Sports came to town."

Alyssa let herself lean against Faith. "Yes, they did. And now my dad and I have to go work there."

Lauren's arm snaked around her shoulders. "I'm so sorry, 'Lys. We'll fix it somehow."

Alyssa hitched out an uneven breath. "H-how?"

"I have no idea, but we're awesome enough to come up with something." The stubbornness in Lauren's voice dared her to suggest otherwise. "We're smart enough to think this through."

"I'm not sure we can. We still need more than eight thousand dollars."

"We can find that," Lauren insisted.

"That's a lot of money to us." Alyssa flushed, shame clawing its way back up her throat. "And my dad isn't the type to ask friends for money. In fact, I think he's given up already. Look, I'm sad right now, but I'll be okay. Dad got me a for-sure job at Top Sports. I'll swallow my pride, work there this summer, and make a pile of money off the enemy."

Lauren stiffened, and Alyssa knew her friend had *a lot* to say, but for once, Lauren held her tongue. Instead, she patted Alyssa's back. "Practice with me."

"I'm not going to camp," Alyssa said, wondering if Lauren had missed that part.

"Maybe, maybe not." Lauren tightened the ribbons on her pointe shoes. "I practice better with you. And who knows? Maybe the camp offers a scholarship."

Alyssa knew they didn't—she'd checked into it a year ago—but she was glad enough to have Lauren talking to her again that she nodded. "Let me go change."

And who knew? Maybe dancing would ease the ache in her heart that had nothing to do with Swing Away.

Buddy barked and danced in circles when Alyssa let herself inside. She stooped to pet his ears, laughing when he flopped onto his back and presented his belly for a rub. "You silly old dog. Who's a good boy? Huh? Is Buddy a good boy?"

Buddy licked her hand, wriggling. She wondered what went through his head sometimes. Dogs had more soul in one paw than most people did in their whole bodies. The only concepts Buddy seemed to care about were Food, Love, Pats, and Walk. And that was fine.

"Chickadee?" Dad's voice came from the living room. "That you?"

"Yeah." She gave Buddy one last scratch and went to find her dad. He was sitting in his armchair, a beer on the side table.

Alyssa paused. Her dad rarely drank during the week. Like, almost never. He'd have a beer or two on the weekends, but that was it. "What's wrong?"

He smiled tiredly at her. His dark hair was mussed, and circles smudged his eyes. "The inspector came by today. He was happy with the nets…but he found that parts of the snack bar weren't to code. It would take another thousand to fix it. 'Dee, I don't know if we can keep the old girl going. Every time we make some ground, we take a step back."

Alyssa clenched her fists. "Sounds like this inspector works for Top Sports."

"He doesn't—everything he pointed out is reasonable." Dad let out a long breath. "I wish I never used your dance money to buy those nets. Maybe Top Sports will buy them from us, so at least I can give the money back to you."

Her pulse pounded in her temples. The defeated tone in his voice only made her angrier. "I don't want my money back, Dad. I want something to go right for us for once."

He stood and came around the chair to face her. Putting his hands on her shoulders, he stared into her eyes. "What have I always said about 'fair'?"

His calm tone was infuriating. "That it only comes around once a year, in the fall, and its job is to sell you corn dogs."

"Right. We'll make it through this. Heck, I'll have a job with health insurance for once." He smiled down at her, brushing a stray tear from her cheek. "I think I'm going to close the shop down on Friday, instead of waiting until next Wednesday. Mom's going to take off work Saturday—how about a family day? It's been a long time since we had one of those."

The fight went out of her, and all Alyssa felt was tired. Exhausted, bone deep. "That…that sounds good. I think I'll go upstairs. I'm worn out."

Dad gave her a hug, and she let herself lean on him a moment, remembering how a "Daddy hug" had fixed everything from a skinned knee to a tough tourney loss when she was younger. Finally, she let go and called, "Buddy dog! Who wants to sleep on my bed?"

A jangle of tags, and Buddy was happily bouncing around her. Most nights he slept in his crate in the kitchen, but when she was feeling extra low, Alyssa liked having him curled up next to her. He usually took his half of the bed up the middle, but tonight she didn't mind.

Buddy followed her down the hall, panting. Every so often, she heard a thump—his tail was wagging so hard, he kept hitting the wall. Alyssa swallowed against a lump in her throat. She hadn't paid enough attention to her Buddy the last few weeks. She hadn't paid enough attention to anything.

Once she and Buddy were settled on her bed, she took a passing glance at her homework and decided it could wait. Everything could… If Swing Away was closing Friday, she needed to help Dad clean out the building, maybe set up an online sale for the machines and such.

And interview with Top Sports.

She sank deeper into her mattress and pulled her quilt up higher. Buddy slid with it and his tail thumped against the bed. "Good boy."

He woofed softly, then settled down. Having her pup with her was comforting, but she was missing something. And she knew exactly who it was.

But Tristan was going to state in four days, and she had work of her own to do. Would it make sense to give him a little time? Or would that make things worse?

How was his hitting doing?

With a sigh, she pulled her phone off the nightstand and texted him.

A: *I misunderstood earlier, and I'm sorry I didn't listen. I know this week's busy for both of us, so maybe we start over next week?*

She put her phone away and closed her eyes, not ready to hear his reply. She'd sleep and let tomorrow take care of itself for once.

Chapter Twenty-Eight

TRISTAN

Alyssa's text came in right as Tristan escaped the dining room, hungry but victorious—he'd managed to pretend he'd eaten a full helping of meatloaf, hiding it in his napkin before throwing it out. Because of the sham, though, he couldn't go to Snap's for a quick burger, so he was stuck going to his room with a half-empty stomach.

He'd felt his phone vibrate in his pocket, but Mom had a "no cell phones" rule at the dinner table. When he saw the message, he sank down on the edge of his bed, not sure how to feel. On one hand, it sounded like Alyssa wanted to give it another go. On the other...*he* wasn't too busy to see her. So why was she putting it off?

He sat, trying to decide how to respond, for a good ten minutes.

I want to start over. Tonight, tomorrow, next week. You tell me when, and I'll be there.

That sounded good, right? Not too desperate? He meant it…every word.

But when he read her text again, he could hear the defeat in her words. Frowning, he texted again:

Is everything else okay? Swing Away?

He didn't really expect to receive an answer, but little bubbles popped up immediately—she was texting him back. He watched and waited, for almost five minutes, until her reply came.

A: *We're closing Friday. Don't worry about it—you have a game to play. You'll do great.*

Their business was closing?

I thought you had another week?

A: *Dad doesn't see any point. It's fine. We're going to be okay.*

Maybe they would be, but she wasn't okay right now.

Can I see you tomorrow?

A long pause.

A: *On the patio, after lunch?*

T: *I'll be there.*

She didn't answer, but he didn't care—she was speaking to him again. That was a good start. He'd figure out the rest… but losing Swing Away hurt. For Alyssa and her family, but for him, too. He'd gotten a little of his mojo back there, and much, much more. It would be like watching his childhood Little

League fields being razed for a parking lot. There had to be something he could do…but what? How could he possibly find enough money to save it? He doubted his parents would help—why would they?

So he'd have to help on his own, and what did he have other than a passable throwing arm and a decent swing… some of the time?

Tristan glanced at himself in the mirror. He'd pulled off his shirt, thinking he was going to change into something more comfortable than the polo his mother liked to see at her dinner table, but hadn't gotten around to putting on a T. He'd been too interested in the text.

Staring at himself, though, he got an idea. A really crazy, flat-out insane idea. He'd need help from a bunch of his teammates, but there was something most of them had that *might* just bring in some cash. Tristan smirked. This could work. Assuming Coach approved it.

He'd have to talk to the guys tomorrow.

Tristan stood outside school the next morning, trying to avoid running into Alyssa before lunch. She wanted space, so he'd give her space. That didn't mean it wasn't going to be torture sitting through class all morning.

Kyle walked up beside him. "Everything okay?"

Tristan shrugged, watching a squirrel try to drag a crust of bread from the trash can to a nearby tree. Persistent bastard… kind of like him. "Alyssa agreed to see me at lunch."

"That good, right?" Kyle asked.

"I hope so. I really like her."

Kyle gave him a "no shit" look. "She's not running away cursing your name. That's a good day, Murrell. Go from there."

"I will." Tristan hoisted his backpack higher on his

shoulder. "Look, I have an idea to help Alyssa's family out with their business. Any chance I can catch you before practice, see what you think?"

"You bet." Kyle glanced over Tristan's shoulder. "Later."

Tristan turned to see Faith coming in from the parking lot. Kyle jogged over to her, taking everything out of her arms but her purse. She smiled up at him in a way that made Tristan a little green with envy. Would Alyssa ever look at *him* like that?

Time would tell. But first, he had to make it through the morning.

That turned out to be harder than he thought. He botched a quiz in Algebra II to start the day. His U.S. history teacher could make the Revolutionary War boring, and today she was talking about the Great Depression…which only made it worse.

After making it through English, spending an entire hour talking about final paper topics, he'd started to doubt everything—the plan for Swing Away, what he'd say to Alyssa, his own swing…everything. He stalked into the cafeteria, not sure if he was angry, sad, hopeful, or disappointed. Probably all four.

Then the cafeteria served him meatloaf. *Meatloaf.*

"That's it," he said when he set his tray on the lunch table. "It feels like the universe might be trying to tell me something."

"I thought you were excited to talk to Alyssa." Dylan frowned. "What changed?"

"I'm scared I'll screw it up, crash and burn." Tristan stared glumly at the table. Someone had etched "Death and all his friends" into the tabletop. Okay, maybe someone had had a worse day than this at one point. "My nerves are scraped raw, that's all."

"Dude, calm down." Dylan pointed a ketchup-covered

French fry at him. "She's not even here yet. You have time to eat something and chill."

Tristan pushed his mostly full tray away. "I'm not hungry."

Dylan snorted. "You haven't been eating enough for a while. I can tell you've lost weight. Not what we need right now. Eat!"

Tristan halfheartedly ate a fry just to shut Dylan up, but it tasted like sawdust. Besides, his stomach wouldn't settle for anything. Alyssa had agreed to see him, but the more he thought about it, the more he realized she hadn't sounded super enthused—was that a bad thing? She said she wanted to start over later, but what did that mean? Square one? Negative four?

"Get out of your own head," Dylan said. "Whatever you're thinking, it's winding you up. Take a breath, man."

Tristan slumped in his chair. "I know, I know."

"This is what happens to you when you bat, too. Your focus is out of whack. There's some kind of demon in there, screwing with your swing." Dylan folded his napkin into a perfect square and lined it up with the edge of the table. "You'll see. Once everything works out with Alyssa, it'll be fine."

But would it work out? "Yeah, sure."

Dylan started to say something, then stopped and pointed. "Believe me or don't. Either way, you're about to find out."

Tristan followed Dylan's line of sight, and there she was. Alyssa was in the cafeteria.

Tristan's heart tried to claw its way up his throat. He couldn't keep his eyes off her. Doubts or not, she was still the most amazing girl in all of Suttonville. Now all he had to do was find a way to convince her he was the right guy.

Chapter Twenty-Nine

ALYSSA

"Hey!" Lauren patted the seat next to her at the lunch table. "Where've you been? I didn't see you after class. I would've waited…"

"No, it's fine. Sorry for ditching you. It's been a weird day." Alyssa set her tray on the table and sank into the chair. She could feel Tristan's eyes on her back. It was strange how something that simple could make her feel both vulnerable and hopeful at the same time. "Jackson pulled me aside when I went to my locker. He apologized."

Lauren raised an eyebrow. "He did? Man, the guys must've scared him bad."

"Yeah, and the apology felt like a 'check the box' kind of thing. 'I'm sorry about the things I said, Alyssa, but you have to understand I was only teasing.'" Alyssa jabbed at her green beans with her fork. "*Only teasing*. Why do guys think they can cover up asshole behavior by calling it teasing?"

"Because some guys are stupid." Lauren flashed her a

bright smile. "But most aren't, and one especially isn't. *That* one hasn't taken his eyes off you since you left the lunch line."

"I know." Alyssa pushed her tray away. Even though there was no point in watching her diet anymore, she didn't think she could eat. Not with her aching stomach. "He wants to meet me."

"What? When?"

Her best friend was far too perky about all this. "As soon as we're done eating."

Lauren looked pointedly at Alyssa's tray. "Seems like that's right now."

"Is he done eating?" Alyssa refused to look over her shoulder at him. Too many feels running around to risk a glance.

"He hasn't taken a bite since you walked in." At Alyssa's frown, Lauren held up her hands. "So maybe I've been spying a little."

Alyssa laid her head on the table in defeat.

Lauren laughed. "And maybe Dylan told me what was going on. Go on, get out of here. I can't take all the angsty tension. Besides, word on the street is that lover boy's swing has been a hot mess the last few days. You need to fix him."

Alyssa sat up. "Fix him? You can't be serious."

Lauren's expression turned stern. "I am serious. You of all people should know that being in a good place makes everything better. You danced perfectly last night. And why? Because you found out that Tristan *does* like you—for real. Now go do the same thing for him."

Alyssa's face grew warm. "I didn't even notice how I danced. Since it doesn't matter anymore, I just…danced."

"You looked gorgeous. On point. Heh. See what I did there?" Lauren gave Alyssa's arm a gentle swat. "So…why are you still here? Go. Before I have to watch Tristan implode over there."

Hands shaking, Alyssa stood slowly, leaving her tray. It was only twelve steps to the patio doors, but she had to make her legs take one step after another. Everything was hyper-focused—the cafeteria lights, the trees outside the glass doors, the blue, blue sky. She'd remember this moment forever, stamped into her mind for the rest of her life.

The day was warm, going on hot and sticky, but she stood in the center of the patio, watching her shadow until Tristan's covered hers.

"Can we talk?" His voice was gravelly. "Please?"

She nodded, not sure she was capable of speaking, and followed him to the little alcove around the corner. Once they were inside, in the shade, she turned around. Tristan stared down at her with those warm brown eyes. He looked so tired, though. Beaten up and down. She knew a little bit about how that felt.

"I'm sorry," she whispered. "I'm sorry I wouldn't listen to you. I should've…I should've trusted you. It's just that…I couldn't believe you would fall for someone like me over someone like Lauren. And when Jackson said—"

"Fuck what Jackson said." The simmering rage in his tone made her take a step back, and Tristan wiped a hand over his face. "Sorry. I'm a little messed up right now, and that's not how I wanted to start this conversation—not with you apologizing to me when you were the one who got hurt, not with me being pissed off at Jackson. I don't care about him. I care about you."

"I know, and I should've believed it." Alyssa took a step toward him, regretting stepping away. He wasn't mad at her, and she didn't want to make him feel worse. "I care about you, too. Enough to tell you something very important."

He searched her face, a flicker of hope in his eyes. "Yeah?"

She took another step toward him and put her hands on his shoulders. "You ready?"

He nodded, and she had to bite back a smile at how serious he was.

"Slow. Down."

Tristan's forehead wrinkled for a second before he got it. He laughed and pulled her into a hug. "With my hitting? I will. With you? No way. I'm not wasting a second with you."

She grinned against his chest. This was where she was supposed to be. "Good, on both counts."

He shifted so they were face-to-face. "Now I'm going to tell *you* something very important. Don't give up on Swing Away—not yet. Trust me, okay?"

Alyssa's heart thumped painfully. "It's sweet of you to say that, but we're out of time and out of options. I'm interviewing at Top Sports on Friday afternoon, trying not to feel like I've sold out."

"You haven't. No matter what happens, you haven't sold out. Not once." Tristan kissed her forehead. "You're one of the hardest working people I've met. And I'm surrounded by athletes all day."

She laughed a little. "Only out of necessity. I can be lazy when I really want to."

He grinned down at her. "Uh-huh? And how often does that happen?"

You've got me there. "Um, about once a year."

"See? I know you."

He reached out and cupped her cheek with his hand. She leaned into it, feeling the calluses on his fingers from baseball. They were the kind of hands that could take care of business and still hold a girl like she was made of porcelain. "So what now?" she asked.

"Now, I kiss you." He tilted her face up to his. "Then I kiss you again."

"Sounds good."

Tristan leaned down to brush her lips with his. Before he

could pull away, Alyssa rose on her tiptoes and kissed him harder, deeper. He groaned and backed her against the wall of the alcove. Who cared if this wasn't a moonlit walk on the beach? The way he was kissing her could set the world on fire.

Every inch of him was pressed against her, and his hand found its way onto bare skin at the small of her back. The troubles of the past few weeks fell away, and all Alyssa wanted to do was relish those calloused fingers drawing circles against her skin. Goose bumps rose on her arms as she slipped her hand under the hem of his shirt. Instead of his back, though, she traced the planes of his stomach. He tensed up, in a good way, his body telling her not to stop. They'd have to, soon, but not yet.

His mouth left hers to kiss its way across her jaw, down her neck, along her collarbone. Alyssa's eyes fell shut, and she leaned against the wall for support, because her knees were going to give any second now. She reached for his face and brought his mouth back to hers, teasing his lips with her tongue.

"Where did they go?" a voice nearby called. Lauren— and she sounded worried. "Do you think everything's okay?"

"Don't know." Dylan's voice was much closer, and Alyssa opened her eyes in time to catch him walking past the opening of the alcove. He stopped and peered in. "Um…I think they're fine."

Alyssa bit her lip as Tristan turned away and struggled for air. Two bright pink spots stained his cheeks, and she'd done a number on his hair. Hers probably looked like she'd been locked in a wind tunnel.

Dylan gave her a salute. "Carry on, then. Lunch bell in five. Plenty of time." He winked and strode out of sight. "Lauren, we can go back in now. Crisis averted."

He whistled as he walked away. Alyssa turned to Tristan, whose shoulders were shaking. She peered at him, worried, just as he burst into laughter. "Oh, man."

She started laughing, too. "Getting caught was inevitable, I guess. Here, I need to fix your hair. It looks like a squirrel's nest."

He bent down so she could finger-comb his hair into place. The whole time she worked on it, he had his eyes closed, like this was the single greatest thing ever to have happened to him. It made her want to kiss him again. But then she'd have to fix his hair again. Endless loop. Not such a bad thing, though.

Tristan brushed a few strands of Alyssa's hair behind her ears. "Okay, I think I'm, um, calm enough to enter society."

Calm enough, huh? Alyssa took his hand. "Then let's go. Oh, and about tomorrow?"

"What about tomorrow?" He straightened his shirt, showing off a flash of stomach that left Alyssa wishing they could ditch class.

"Don't forget to bring a comb." She rose up on tiptoe to whisper in his ear. "You'll need it."

Chapter Thirty

Tristan

Tristan had a lot of trouble concentrating the rest of the day. He kept reliving the moment when Alyssa's fingers met the skin on his stomach, how her skin felt under his lips, how she smelled, tasted…

Yeah, class was a lost cause.

When the final bell rang, he raced to find Alyssa, thinking maybe he could steal a kiss or two before practice. He ran into Lauren instead. She held up a hand. "Whoa, there, tiger."

"I was looking for—"

"Alyssa. I know." Lauren shook her head, smiling. "She has work release last period."

Disappointment flooded his veins. "Damn. I was hoping to—"

"Oh, I know what you were hoping, but you'll need to hit the old pause button. Alyssa's at Swing Away, helping her dad pack things up."

Lauren's smile had faded over that last bit, but Tristan

perked up. "I have an idea to save their business, but I'm going to need help. Is there any way you can stall them? Keep them from closing before the deadline? They have until next Friday, and I need the time."

"Not sure I can, but I'll try." Her eyes narrowed. "What's your plan?"

He was going to be late for practice, so he sketched out the details as fast as he could. "We play all weekend, but Sunday night should work. What do you think?"

Lauren was doubled over, laughing. "Even if it doesn't raise enough money, I'm in. And Tristan?"

"Yeah?"

She pointed a finger at him. "That swing of yours better be golden."

He waved at her, then ran down the hall to the locker room. He had some plotting to do.

When he made it to the dugout, Dylan was having a very animated discussion with Kyle, who was laughing so hard he had to stop and wipe his eyes. Dylan mimed looking around a corner and covered his mouth in exaggerated shock.

"Dennings!" Tristan called. "Stop messing around, get out there, and throw me a changeup."

Dylan shot Kyle a look, who nodded. Dylan shrugged and grabbed his glove and a ball. "I live to serve, asshat."

Tristan trotted up the stairs behind him and went to the batter's box for a few warm-up swings. So what if he hadn't done his sprints, or stretched...or anything? He'd already had one hell of a cardio workout today, and he hadn't cooled down yet.

"Ready?" Dylan called.

"Ready."

Dylan wound up and pitched, and the scariest changeup Tristan had ever seen his friend throw hurtled toward him.

Slow down.

Tristan let out a breath and swung.

The bat connected so well, he felt it in his wrists. The ball sailed up, up, up…and over the scoreboard.

Dylan's eyebrows had disappeared under his hair. "Do it again!"

Fastball. Curve. Another changeup. Tristan smashed every single one for at least a base hit.

By the time he was done, the guys in the dugout had started clapping. He turned and bowed, then jogged over to Kyle, who was warming up in the on-deck circle.

"Looks like your mojo's back," Kyle said.

"I think so." Tristan laughed. "Funny how the 'other thing' makes this stuff easier."

Kyle snorted. "I heard about you and Alyssa making out behind a wall on the patio. Sounds like you're good now."

"Yeah. But there's still a problem—Alyssa's dad is about to lose his business."

Kyle stopped stretching. "It's that bad?"

"Yeah. They need eight or ten grand to keep it open. I have an idea, but I'll need you to agree to it first. It's a little weird."

Kyle took a practice swing. "I've heard that once before. Last time worked out pretty okay, so let's hear it."

Before Tristan even finished, Kyle had gathered half the team together, so he had to repeat everything. Most of them were nodding with interest. One sophomore flexed his biceps—not too bad for a shorter kid. "I'm in."

"We all are." Dylan pushed through the crowd. "And, from now on, external batting practice is at Swing Away."

"Assuming they stay open," Tristan said. "But I think if all of us help them, they might."

"What are you guys doing?" Coach bellowed. "Why aren't you out running sprints?"

The whole team scattered to start drills, and Tristan joined them, feeling better than he had for a while.

The rest of the week passed too fast. He sneaked kisses from Alyssa whenever he could, and she and Lauren joined them at their lunch table. For a while, he thought Dylan might be developing a crush on Lauren, but it turned out they were just good friends. It was hard for the three of them to keep Alyssa in the dark about their plans, but Tristan had insisted.

"If this doesn't work, I don't want her to be disappointed, okay?" he told the team at practice Wednesday. "No one can tell her. When we spread the word, make sure everyone knows it's a surprise."

So far, no one had blabbed. He hated how drawn Alyssa looked, though. He took her outside after lunch on Thursday. "The team's leaving tonight. Our game is at four tomorrow, and Coach wants to practice early. Will you be all right while I'm gone?"

She reached for his hand. "I'll be fine. I begged Dad to stay open through the weekend, so I'll be at Swing Away as much as I can. That will give me a chance to say good-bye."

His heart constricted, making his chest ache. "I want to think it'll all be okay. Maybe you can convince him to stay open until next Friday."

"I want to, but he's pretty defeated. Top Sports wants him to start in two weeks. Staying open longer means less time to close things down." Alyssa brushed some hair back from her face. The wind was strong today, out of the west, and it was blowing her curls around. He loved it. "And I interview there Friday afternoon."

He took her other hand and faced her. "Is that what you want?"

She shrugged. "I'm qualified, and it pays a dollar an hour

more than Dad does. It's hard not to see them as the enemy, though."

"Do whatever you think will make you happiest." He leaned in to give her a quick kiss. "That's all I want—to see you happy. Because you've made me happy, too."

At that, he finally coaxed a real smile out of her. She grabbed the front of his T-shirt and pulled him down into a more lingering kiss.

"PDA!" a weary teacher called.

Tristan sighed against Alyssa's mouth. "I was hoping for a good-luck kiss, too."

Alyssa grabbed his hand and dragged him to the alcove. They barely made it around the wall before she gave him a fierce, searing kiss that left him lightheaded.

"Will that work?" she asked, all innocence.

"Yeah." If his math teacher asked what two times four was, he doubted he'd be able to puzzle it out. Not after that. "But maybe one more…just in case?"

She laughed and kissed him again. "You're going to be fine. No, *more* than fine. Listen to me—you're going to be a goddamn hero. Understood?"

"Yes, ma'am." He ran his hands through her hair. "And when we get back, I have a little surprise for you. Are you free Sunday evening?"

She eyed him suspiciously. "I'm pretty sure I will be. I don't plan to start at Top Sports until school lets out. I want some time off. What kind of surprise?"

"A surprise." He grinned when she gave him an annoyed look. "Something to look forward to."

"Okay." She didn't sound too sure. "Good luck this weekend."

He pulled her into a hug. "Thanks. But I'm pretty sure I have all the luck I need right here."

Chapter Thirty-One

Alyssa

Friday was way too quiet. Alyssa kept glancing at Tristan's empty chair at lunch, feeling just as empty. Dad had told her to dismantle the two broken pitching machines last night... and it had felt too much like giving up. Plus, the assistant manager at Top Sports had called her on the way to school to make sure they were on for the interview.

So far, this Friday was shaping up to be more like a Monday.

"He'll be back soon." Lauren gave her an encouraging smile that she quickly turned on Faith. "You, too, mopey face."

Faith rolled her eyes. "This is the first time Kyle's been gone since we started going out. I didn't think it would be a big deal...but it is. He sent me some flowers, though. Mom called to say they'd been delivered to the house."

Lauren mimed gagging. "These guys are so sweet I'm getting a cavity."

Alyssa had to laugh. Faith and Kyle could be a little

annoying. Cute, but oh-my-God-stop-making-googly-eyes annoying.

"Hey, remember that you were caught with your hand up Tristan's shirt, missy. If anyone gets to be tickled by this situation, it's me." Lauren jabbed a thumb at her chest. "I'm still boyfriend-less."

"You had your hand up his shirt?" Faith leaned forward. "I didn't hear about that."

Alyssa groaned. Her face was so flushed, it felt sunburned. "I think we should focus on finding Lauren a boyfriend."

"She's deflecting," Faith said.

"Totally." Lauren tossed a napkin at Alyssa. "And before you ask, I'm not going out with Dylan. He's a friend is all. And he's also a little too…uptight for me."

"Pitcher," Alyssa said, and Faith nodded.

"Anyhoo, I heard Jackson still has his arms, and he'll be pitching today." Lauren took a bite out of her muffin. "He better not screw this up, or else."

"He's arrogant enough to do fine. I'm more worried about Tristan." Alyssa scooped up a forkful of salad, stared at it, and dropped it on her tray. "I wish I didn't have that interview today. I'd rather be in San Antonio."

"I'm going tomorrow if they win tonight," Faith said. "You should come with me. Road trip!"

Alyssa's shoulders rounded under the weight of everything else she had to do. She wished—wished—she could go, but that wasn't possible. "Thanks for the offer, but my dad said something about family time this weekend. Plus, we have a lot to do at Swing Away."

"If you change your mind, let me know." Faith gave her a secretive smile. "What are you doing Sunday? If the guys win, there's going to be a big celebration thing at the baseball fields."

"I'm definitely going to that." Was that the surprise

Tristan had mentioned? It would be so great if the guys *did* win. The entire time she'd known Tristan, he'd been a little stressed. What would he be like when the pressure was off?

What would he *kiss* like when the pressure was off?

"Lord, I don't even want to know what you're thinking," Lauren said, waving her fork. "I better go. I have some things to do before class."

Faith checked her watch and yelped. "Oh! Me, too."

"Like what?" Alyssa looked between them. What was so important that they'd leave fifteen minutes into lunch period?

"School project," Lauren said.

"Drama stuff," Faith said at the same time.

Alyssa leaned back in her chair. "You two are acting weird. What's going on?"

Lauren flashed her a bright smile. "Not a thing. Enjoy your lunch!"

The two girls hurried out of the cafeteria, heads close together. Definitely suspicious, and it had something to do with *her*—Alyssa was sure of it. But what were they up to?

"You have a lot of experience," Ms. Compton said. "Even mechanical—that's impressive."

The assistant manager for sports programming at Top Sports turned out to be younger than Alyssa imagined. *All* the managers, including the GM, were younger than her dad by ten years or more. What would it be like for him, starting over in a place like this?

"A place like this" was spotless, gleaming, and plastic. The entire complex oozed money, but not in a good way. The batting cages were high-tech, with the best pitching machines on the market and perfect nets. Ms. Compton told her they were replaced every year. "Whether they need it or not," she'd said. "We want to preserve the aesthetic."

Which was a fancy way of saying "we want to be newer and shinier than everyone else."

Now, Alyssa sat across from Ms. Compton in a small office in the main building. Outside the door, employees bustled to the bar—a full bar, that included a limited restaurant menu—or to the driving ranges, or the cages, or wherever else the thirty-seven people on shift went. The place was *huge*, and intimidating.

Alyssa could barely control her distaste. Her blood pulsed with helpless anger. This place was here to put the bowling alley on Main, the driving range off Porter Road, and Swing Away out of business. Pure and simple. Top Sports management had seen the money in Suttonville and come running.

"So you'll be managing a staff of three on every shift," Ms. Compton was saying. Her sky-blue polo, with TOP SPORTS embroidered over her heart, strained across her chest, and her smile looked like something out of the Miss Texas pageant. That was another thing—most of the staff looked as plastic and pretty as the complex.

Alyssa gritted her teeth. "Mostly high school students?"

"No, the majority of our staff is eighteen and up. You're the youngest person we've considered hiring." Ms. Compton's smile twitched. "But your father is very persuasive."

Someone didn't like the conditions of Dad's employment. Alyssa could see why—she didn't fit the Top Sports mold. And there was no way she was capping her teeth for a job that paid eleven dollars an hour. "I'm very mature for my age."

"That's what I hear. Well, your schedule in the summer will be very busy. We require supervisors to work no less than thirty hours a week during the summer. You will probably close some nights and open the next day on occasion." Ms. Compton's smile turned into a smirk. "New supervisors pick shifts last. Seniority, you know."

That wasn't what her dad had said. He'd said she would have a flexible schedule. "How late do you close?" Alyssa looked over Ms. Compton's shoulder at the huge lights lining the edges of the complex. "And when do you open?"

"In the summer, we open at eight and close at midnight." Ms. Compton steepled her fingers. "Surely that won't be a problem, right?"

Alyssa met her gaze. "So, I'll have less than eight hours between shifts in the summer. Doesn't that violate child labor laws?"

"No." Ms. Compton's fake smile faded. "You're seventeen. The law says you can work the same hours as an adult. And you will be treated just like every other supervisor who was hired directly."

Alyssa heard what she wasn't saying—Dad had talked Compton's boss into hiring her, but that didn't mean the other assistant managers had to like it.

That didn't mean Alyssa had to like it, either. Flipping burgers or making smoothies would be better than this. So what if she loved being around batting cages? Losing Swing Away didn't mean Top Sports was her only option, and she had to stop thinking about it that way. This place was giving her hives, and Ms. Compton reminded her of a fembot. If she had to get up every morning this summer and come here, how much damage would be done? Who would she be by the time school started?

No, she couldn't do it.

Alyssa stood. "I thank you for the time, Ms. Compton, but I prefer not to sell out at this time. I'm sure you'll find a willing college student for my position. Have a nice day."

"What? Wait, where are you—"

Alyssa shut the door between them and leaned against the wall. Dad was probably going to come home wearing a very stern expression, but it would be worth it. She'd been practical her whole life, and lately that had caused nothing but trouble. Not anymore. From now on, she was going to sing with the car windows rolled down, walk barefoot outside, and look for a job she could do without feeling like she needed to shower.

And she was going to do it her own way.

Chapter Thirty-Two

TRISTAN

"Good catch out there." Coach slugged Tristan's shoulder as he jogged down the dugout steps. "Now I want a base hit."

It was the bottom of the third, and while Jackson was pitching well, a rare error at shortstop had allowed Conroe a run in the second. Tristan's first at-bat had been a pop fly to center field to end the first. He'd left two men on—two men who could've put the Sentinels in the lead.

He swallowed his nerves, nodded to Coach, and climbed up to the on-deck circle to take a few practice swings while Conroe's pitcher warmed up. The ump signaled time, and Tristan walked to the batter's box.

"Now hitting for the Sentinels, number twenty-seven, Tristan Murrell," the announced said over the speakers.

Tristan took a deep breath. *Please throw a grapefruit.* He stepped in and raised his bat.

The pitcher wound up. In a blink, a curveball raced toward Tristan. He swung.

"Strike!" the umpire yelled.

Shit. Shit, shit, shit. Tristan stepped out and rolled his shoulders. He could do this. He needed to slow down, just like Alyssa said.

He stepped back in. The next pitch was a wild changeup. "Ball!"

Okay, he could live with a walk. A walk would be fine. The pitcher watched the catcher, picking the next pitch.

A fastball, right down the middle.

"Strike!"

Tristan stepped out again and squeezed his eyes shut. He tried to remember how it felt when Alyssa kissed him out of the blue that first Sunday. How his brain reset back to caveman and his muscles took over.

He stepped back in, breathed. Another fastball, gorgeous, begging to be whacked over the fence. Tristan swung with his entire body.

"Strike!"

Once he stopped the momentum of his swing, Tristan stamped a cleat into the dirt, frustrated. He stalked into the dugout to sympathetic pats and calls of "You'll get it next time!" He ignored all of them and flopped onto the bench. He should've been up there egging Sawyer on, but he didn't have the energy.

Dylan came over and sat next to him. "Dude."

"I don't want to hear it." Tristan rested his face in his hands. "I thought I had it back. I thought maybe Alyssa was my good luck charm or something. But I can't hit anything."

Ting!

Cheers roared from the crowd, and Dylan hopped up to look. "Sawyer crushed a homer. Tied us up." He came back to the bench. "Enough wallowing. Suck it up, buttercup. The freshmen are looking at you, and you're acting like a grouchy six-year-old."

Tristan pushed himself up. Dylan was right. He went over to congratulate Kyle as he jogged down the steps. "Good job."

"Thanks. Now, we sort you out, and we'll have ourselves a ball game."

"I'm going to try."

"Good."

Kyle went to grab a drink, and Tristan stared at the team. They were so happy, so pumped to be here. Suttonville's first state championship team…but only if they won today.

And he had to play a part in that. He was the leadoff hitter in the heart of the order. He had to get it together, fast.

"Bottom of the seventh, one out. Next up, Tristan Murrell of the Sentinels. Two men on, one out, with the Tigers holding a one-run lead."

The announcer's voice boomed through the stadium, reminding Tristan this was his last shot. If he didn't get it done, it would be down to Kyle. Tristan had hit a single in the sixth, but that was the end of his production for the day. He needed to be a hero.

Conroe's closer was one of the best bullpen pitchers in the state of Texas. He hadn't blown a save in two years.

No pressure.

Tristan rolled his neck as he walked to the batter's box. He knew what the guy would throw—either a mean curveball or a fastball that could outrace a Corvette. That didn't make it any easier to approach the plate. His stomach cramped.

You're in your own head, man. Stop it. It's just another pitcher. Tristan squared his shoulders and raised his bat. Just another pitcher.

The first pitch, a fastball to rival one of Dylan's, flew by before Tristan even got his bearings.

"Strike!"

Okay, fine. No big deal. He was sizing the guy up, was all.

Another fastball. This time Tristan swung and caught nothing but air.

The umpire threw the pitcher a new ball, and he looked it over before smirking at Tristan. As if to say, *What are you going to do about it, loser?*

Tristan tightened his hands on his bat.

The pitcher wound up and threw him a curveball.

"Strike!"

Tristan let out a ragged breath. The guys on first and second jogged back to their bases to tag up. He'd blown it, big time.

"Stop letting it get into your head," Sawyer hissed in his ear as he made his way to the plate.

Tristan kept walking and slunk into the dugout to watch. The pitcher gave Kyle the same smirk. Kyle returned it. *Improved* on it.

And on the first pitch—the first damn pitch—Kyle slammed that fastball into deep right. It dropped into the corner, and the outfielder had to run after it, giving plenty of time for their guys on first and second to sprint around the bases…and win the game.

"Did you guys *see* that?" Jackson was waving his arms around. "The closer's face. Oh my God, I'm taking that sight to the grave!"

The team was bouncing around the locker room like kangaroos on meth. Coach had even let them spray each other with soda cans—after lining the room with plastic sheeting.

Tristan was the only one not celebrating. He sat on the bench, staring at the nameplate on his locker. He knew he'd been helpful on defense, especially catching the final out in the seventh and saving two runs from scoring, but he couldn't call it a success until he came through with his batting when it mattered. People were going to start calling him a choker.

He glanced over at Kyle, who was on the phone, laughing. He looked like he'd won the lottery. At least someone had come through for the team.

Coach came in, telling them to knock off the noise and clean up. "Bus leaves in twenty whether you monsters are on it or not!"

Tristan grabbed his towel, but Coach stopped him on the way to the showers. "Hold up a minute, Murrell."

Once the locker room was clear, Coach said, "I don't want to see another performance like this tomorrow."

"I'm trying, Coach. I've been working on my swing—"

"I don't mean the hitting. I mean the sulking. If you want to be my team captain next year, you need to have some professionalism, young man." Coach glowered down at him. "This is a *team*, Murrell, and leadership is required. If you do this again tomorrow, I'm giving the captain position to Dennings. Period."

Tristan swallowed against the tide of shame constricting his throat. "Yes, sir."

"All right. Hit the shower." Tristan turned to go, but Coach stopped him. "And, Murrell? No matter how much I like winning, it's just a game. It's supposed to be fun, kid."

He left the locker room, but Tristan stood frozen. If it was supposed to be fun, why did he feel like his heart had been ripped out and stomped on?

Shaking his head, he stalked into the showers.

Chapter Thirty-Three

ALYSSA

"I'm home!" Alyssa tore through the house, looking for her parents. She'd gone straight to Faith's after her interview, and they'd listened to the game. Kyle had won it for them, but it sounded like Tristan was unraveling. After the game, Kyle had called Faith and told her they had a problem.

And she was the only one who could fix it.

"Where is everyone?"

"In the kitchen!" her mom called, and Buddy tore around a corner to jump on Alyssa's legs.

"Good boy!" She scratched him but didn't stop moving. Her parents were sitting at the kitchen table, the remnants of spaghetti on plates in front of them.

Dad perked up when he saw her. "How was the interview?"

"I'm not working there." She said it with as much force as she could. "I *can't* work there. Dad, you do what you need to do, but I'm going to find another job."

Her dad's mouth opened, but Alyssa held up a hand. "I know that's not what you wanted to hear, but it's what I want. And that's not why I'm here, anyway."

"But, 'Dee…you love working cages." Dad's forehead was creased with worry. "Are you sure?"

"Yes. Very." Alyssa crossed her arms over her chest. "Now, about that other thing."

"What's up, honey?" Mom asked.

If she wasn't mistaken, there was a hint of pride in Mom's voice. Did she feel the same way about Top Sports? That was something to figure out later, though. "I'm going to San Antonio with Faith. We're leaving at four in the morning."

"Why on earth?" Mom turned a bewildered look on Dad. "Do you know?"

"State baseball championship. Did Suttonville win, then?" Dad asked.

"Yes, but Tristan—the guy I've been helping with batting—he's coming unglued. That's what Faith's boyfriend told her. I need to go down there. He *needs* me, Dad."

"What on earth? I'm sure he's fine…" Mom's forehead was creased with worry. "Tearing off for San Antonio at the spur of the moment isn't like you."

"Maybe not, but maybe I want to stop being so practical for a while. I want to be spontaneous." She threw up her hands. "Dad, you understand what I'm saying, right?"

A little smile played at the corners of Dad's mouth. "Are you his batting coach or his muse?"

Alyssa mustered the most serious expression she could. "Both. I'm both. The game starts at eleven thirty, and we need to be there in time for batting practice at the stadium."

Dad picked up a book from the kitchen table. "Have fun."

"Grant…you're okay with her tearing across the state on a wild hair like this?" Mom shook her head. "What is going on with you two?"

"We're living the dream, Mom." Alyssa kissed her on the top of the head. "I need to go pack a few things. I'm spending the night at Faith's so I don't wake you up in the morning."

As she hurried from the room, she heard her mom ask her dad, "Are you really okay with this?"

"I'm totally fine with it." Dad chuckled. "Far be it from me to watch our high school lose state because a hitter's lucky charm is a few hundred miles away."

Buddy chased Alyssa through the house, wagging his tail and yipping. Her excitement was catching, it seemed, and when she ran into her room, he hopped onto the bed, dancing in circles. Alyssa grabbed him and hugged him around the neck. "We're going to do this, boy. For once, I'm going to fix something and see it work."

Alyssa's heart had been in her throat the entire time she listened to the game on the radio. TV hadn't picked up the semifinals, but they'd broadcast tomorrow's championship game. Tristan had only had one hit today, and Kyle's call from the locker room had confirmed everything she'd worried about.

"He's a mess," Kyle had said over speakerphone to the two of them. "He's sitting by himself in the locker room, like someone gut-punched him."

"Poor Tristan," Faith murmured. "What should we do?"

"The only thing we can," Alyssa said. "Give me a ride to San Antonio."

Kyle had laughed at that. "Good idea. Batting practice is at ten thirty. That will be the only time he'll be able to see you before the game."

So now she was throwing clothes, makeup, and her glove into a bag while her dog bounced on her bed. This was the craziest thing she'd ever done, traveling halfway across the state to see after a boy, but lately "crazy" had been her middle name. And she liked it.

Buddy gave her cheek a lick, almost like he was telling her good luck. "Thanks, boy. Hold down the fort while I'm gone."

She gave him one last pat, then hurried down the stairs. "I'm going!"

"Text when you get there!" Mom called.

"Tell that kid to shape up!" Dad added.

Alyssa laughed. After telling Top Sports no, a huge weight had come off her shoulders, and she felt light enough to fly. "You bet I will!"

"There are a lot of people here," Faith said as they pushed through the crowd on the concourse.

"Yeah, and probably some scouts, too." Based on the sounds of balls being struck by bats, they'd made it to the stadium right on time. "We need to fight our way to the front."

They found the nearest tunnel and weaved through people standing around chatting. At the end, a grumpy-looking older woman stood with a chain pulled across the entrance. "Seating opens in ten minutes." Her voice was pinched and sour, like she'd said that a hundred times already.

Alyssa looked helplessly at Faith. "Please, ma'am, our boyfriends play for Suttonville. We just want to say hi."

"Seating opens in ten minutes." The lady gave her a flat look. "No exceptions."

"Ma'am...it's an emergency." Faith's eyes had gone wide, and she was laying a Texas drawl on thick. "See, Alyssa's boyfriend is having some trouble with his glove. She brought him one from home. We need to sneak in for a sec, hand it off, and we'll come right back. Promise."

The woman's features softened. Faith had that effect on people — Alyssa needed to learn how she did it. She pulled the glove from her backpack, hoping the lady couldn't tell a softball glove from a baseball glove. "Please?"

The woman rolled her eyes but smiled at Faith. "Oh, all right. Just this once."

"Thank you!" Faith shot her a dazzling smile, and the chain was lifted away.

A moment later, they heard, "Seating opens in nine minutes."

"But those girls went," a man said.

"Emergency," the woman snapped.

Faith hid a laugh behind her hand. "I'm such a liar."

"Who cares? It worked." Alyssa scanned the field. Suttonville was practicing on the third-base side. "Come on."

Tristan was standing on the foul line, about halfway down from third, talking to Kyle. The girls scrambled between rows, working their way down. If Kyle saw them, he didn't show it.

Pausing to gulp down a breath, Alyssa smoothed back her hair, then trotted down the last few steps. "Excuse me. I'm looking for a baseball player."

Tristan froze. "Is there a girl behind me?"

Kyle laughed. "Yes, dumbass. There's a girl behind you."

"Okay. I was worried I was hearing voices or something." Tristan turned, and a slow, sweet smile spread across his face. "Kaplan, what the hell are you doing here?"

She leaned on the wall separating the stands from the field, hoping her skirt hadn't blown up in back during her wild dash through the seats. "I heard you needed a batting coach."

In one quick move, Tristan vaulted the wall and wrapped his arms around her. His coach shouted something inarticulate, but Tristan didn't listen. "I need *you*."

Then he was kissing her, and Alyssa knew, just knew, everything was going to be fine.

Chapter Thirty-Four

"I can't believe you're here." Tristan hugged Alyssa tight. "I thought you were working at Swing Away all weekend."

She laughed against his collarbone. "You might need to stop squeezing so hard if you want me to talk."

"Oh, sorry." He let her out of the hug but held her at arm's length, still reeling with surprise. "How'd you get here?"

Alyssa pointed at Faith, who was leaning against the wall, smiling at Kyle. "We listened to the game last night. I thought you might need some encouragement." Her cheeks flushed pink. "And I missed you some, too."

She missed him. *Now those are words I've been waiting to hear.* "I'm glad you came." He kissed her cheek. "So glad."

"Murrell!" Coach barked. "What are you doing up there? Come down here and hit!"

Tristan jumped guiltily. "I, uh, better go. See you after? I have to ride the team bus home, but we'll probably have a few minutes before we leave."

"Murrell! You, too, Sawyer. Tell the ladies good-bye!" Coach sounded like he was about to start frothing at the mouth. "Now!"

"Coming!" Tristan grinned at Alyssa. "Wish me luck!"

"Trust me—I already have." She smiled. "I'll cheer loud."

His heart swelled like it was going to come out of his chest and dance. "I believe you."

He jumped the wall and jogged over to the batting station. "Sorry. I had to see about something."

Coach made a face. "First Sawyer leaving in the middle of a game a few months ago, and now I catch you smooching some girl in the stands before the championship. I'm not running eHarmony!"

"Did he say eHarmony?" Dylan snickered. "Coach is old."

"I heard that!" Coach stomped off to yell at some freshman, and Tristan took his place in the makeshift batter's box.

An assistant coach stood behind a protective screen that was lower on one side so he could pitch. He'd been a pitcher for Texas A&M fifteen years ago and could still throw an eighty-mile-per-hour heater when he felt like it. Dylan stopped warming up to watch... This was almost as helpful for him as it was for the batters.

"Tristan Murrell!" Alyssa called. "You better hit that ball!"

Grinning, he raised his bat and waited for the pitch. A slider—and a damn good one at that. Tristan let out a quick breath and swung.

Ting!

Dylan let out a whoop. "That's a double!"

"Told you so!" Alyssa's voice held a thread of laughter. "Now do it again!"

And he did.

"Having her here really helps." Dylan sounded almost dumbfounded by that. "Here am I thinking that it's routine, practice, focus…and you hit because you're a lovesick bastard."

"Whatever works," Kyle said, breezing past them to grab a bottle of water from the cooler in the corner. "Even if it's lucky socks."

"Hey, if Bishop turns another double play today, I'll deal with smelly socks." Dylan rubbed his hands together nervously. "Come on, it's time for the anthem."

They filed onto the field. Butterflies fluttered in Tristan's stomach, but they felt like the good kind—the kind that said he was ready to play. Alyssa was somewhere in the stands, watching. She'd come all this way to see him, and he'd damn well be a hero for her.

The northern team was visiting this year, meaning Suttonville had to bat first against Ronald Reagan High. The Rattlers had their best pitcher on the mound today—this wasn't like the big leagues where you had to win four of seven to take the World Series. Today it was one and done. Win, or go home in second place.

Their pitcher proved his skill in the first inning. He shut down the first three batters, a foul ball the only contact anyone made.

Dylan shot the pitcher an icy gaze. "My turn."

"Light 'em up." Tristan grabbed his glove and ran to the outfield. A piercing whistle echoed from the crowd.

As Kyle jogged by, he said, "Jesus. I think that was your girlfriend."

Probably—Tristan didn't have any trouble believing it. He waved in the general direction of the whistle and hunkered down for the fight.

Dylan struck out the first batter without a bit of trouble. The second batter hit a long foul ball that Kyle somehow ran down for an out. The third batter came up and hit a tiny blooper that went through the second baseman's legs. Tristan sped toward the ball, scooped it up, and threw, but it was too late. Their man was on first.

Fine. They had two outs. They'd catch the next one.

The fourth batter came to the plate. He was huge, probably six-five, with arms like tree trunks. Tristan watched Dylan wipe his hand on his pants. Once, twice, three times.

Not good. Dylan became ritualistic when things weren't going his way. Tristan backed up, almost to the track at the back of the field. Out of the corner of his eye, he saw Kyle did, too. If Dylan was nervous, they had a problem.

First pitch, a curveball, low. The guy stood there and watched it go by.

The second pitch was in the strike zone, mostly, and the batter swung, clipping the edge of the ball and sending it like a cannon shot into the stands. The crowd gasped… Someone had probably been hit.

Okay, one-one count. Dylan paced on the mound after catching a fresh ball. The batter waggled his bat, looking completely comfortable. Tristan exchanged a glance with Kyle and took one more step back toward the wall.

The third pitch rolled off Dylan's hand—a fastball that hiccupped a little and sailed straight down the middle. Tristan barely had time to think *oh shit*, before the ball had left the bat in a high arc.

He ran to the left, trying to get under it, but the ball wasn't coming down. He scrambled backward and jumped. The ball lipped the edge of his glove and fell behind the wall.

Two-run shot, bottom of the first.

"Damn it!" Tristan slid down the wall. "I had it!"

"Good try, man." Kyle shook his head. "Not even Nelly

Cruz could've caught that."

The Rattlers finished running the bases while the Suttonville catcher went to the mound to calm Dylan down. They whispered behind the catcher's glove for a moment as the next batter warmed up. Finally, the ump called the catcher back, and play resumed.

This time, Dylan threw a fastball that had the batter swinging for the fences...and missing. Two more, and he struck him out. The damage was done, though. They needed to make up some runs.

And Tristan was leading off the second.

Chapter Thirty-Five

Alyssa held her breath as Tristan made his way to the on-deck circle to warm up. The Reagan pitcher was better than Dylan, and if the Sentinels wanted to win, they'd have to do it by hitting smart and fielding smarter. She was convinced they had the fielding part down—Tristan had almost saved that clear homer in the first—but would they hit off this guy?

Faith patted her arm. "He looks good."

He did—his stance was nice and loose, bat poised at a good angle. He also looked great in his uniform. She hadn't thought about that during the mad rush to San Antonio, but the sight of him in those baseball pants made the five-hour drive worth it. The short sleeves were a bonus, too.

"Now batting for the Sentinels, Tristan Murrell," the announcer said.

Tristan shook out his arms and walked to the batter's box. Alyssa reached for Faith's hand. "Come on. You've got this."

The pitcher wound up. Slider. Tristan watched it go by,

and Alyssa let out a sigh of relief.

"Ball!"

The pitcher had been testing the waters a bit, she was sure of it. Hell, she'd done the same thing a few times. Throw something a little low, a little outside, and you might get lucky with a missed call by the ump, or a batter who'd swing at anything.

The pitcher watched the catcher, shaking his head once, then again. Finally, he nodded and cupped the ball in his glove. Tristan shifted his weight.

The pitch came—fastball. Tristan swung and made contact. The ball flew into the outfield, rolling far into the corner. Alyssa leapt to her feet screaming, "Run! Run!"

Tristan cleared first base and barreled toward second. The throw was coming, so he slid under the second baseman's glove, missing a tag by inches.

"Safe!"

Alyssa jumped up and down. "A double! He hit a double!"

Faith shot to her feet next to Alyssa. "Kyle Sawyer, you bring him home!"

Kyle, who'd been stalking to the batter's box, stopped. He actually *stopped* and winked up at Faith, who blew him a kiss.

Alyssa shook her head. "You two really are kind of disgusting. You know that, right?"

Faith's expression was intense. "If he hits a homer, you'll thank me."

"If he hits a homer, I'll kiss him on the mouth."

"No, that's my job." Faith's eyes didn't leave Kyle. "Come on, baby. Show off for everyone."

The first pitch was low and outside. What was it with Reagan's pitcher and throwing the same pitch every time he felt out a batter? She wished she could text that bit of intel to the coach, but he had to see it himself. One of these days, a batter was going to get wise and find a way to hit that pitch.

The next pitch was a really sweet changeup. Kyle caught the ball on the tip of his bat, sending it just foul of the first-base line.

Kyle shook it off and waited for the pitcher to eye Tristan's position. Tristan trotted back to second—he'd taken a pretty wide lead back there. Finally, the pitcher threw his third pitch.

Fastball, down the middle.

Ting!

Faith started screaming and waving her arms as the ball sailed up, up, up, and over the fence. The crowd roared, but Alyssa only had eyes for Tristan. He jogged around third to home with his head held high. Kyle followed, and half the team met him outside the dugout for fist bumps and high fives.

Faith threw her arms around Alyssa. "They did it!"

Alyssa hugged her back. "They did."

And in a way, she and Faith had helped.

"It's the top of the ninth, and after a wild first few innings, we're tied up in what's become a pitchers' duel here at the state championship," the commentator said on the radio app Alyssa had downloaded to her phone. "It's three-three between the Rattlers and the Sentinels, giving us extra baseball. For the listeners at home, high school teams have seven-inning games, but in the case of a tie, they keep playing, and these teams are showing no signs of letting up. Batting next, we start with the top of Suttonville's order. At least one of these batters needs to find a way on base so the Sentinels' sluggers—Murrell and Sawyer—have a chance to bring someone home."

"Yeah, Bob, they need smart play to start off the inning, and a hero to end it," the other commentator said. "Now, Reagan is one of those fortunate teams to have a solid pitcher in closing position. Suttonville isn't that deep and will be looking for Dennings to finish the job since their third pitcher is on the DL. That's a tall order."

"Definitely."

Alyssa turned the radio off. She didn't want to hear the odds. This was too much of a nail-biter, and she'd learned long ago not to listen too closely to predictions. That's one thing her dad taught her—baseball had as many variables as the weather, and, like meteorologists, commentators were only right about 30 percent of the time.

No, she wanted to see Tristan hit one to the fences. He'd hit two other singles, including one to bring in their third run, before the pitcher had hunkered down. On the plus side, Dylan had hunkered down, too. He went out there, inning after inning, and did his job. So now they had a nail-biter.

"Stop chewing on your fingers," Faith said, snatching Alyssa's hand away from her mouth.

Alyssa clutched her hands together in her lap. "I can't help it. I'm freaking out a little."

"Me, too." Faith gazed at the field. "We need a base runner. Hopefully two."

Reagan's closer finished warming up, and the first batter took his place. The first pitch was a fastball—fast and straight from a guy whose arm was still fresh. The batter didn't even twitch.

"Strike!"

"This could be a problem." Alyssa's fingers found their way to her mouth again.

Faith swatted at her. "Stop."

The next pitch, a solid curve, was hittable. The batter made contact, but the ball didn't have any distance and the left fielder made an easy catch. Out number one.

The second batter did even worse. He hit a pop fly on the very first pitch. After only three pitches, their closer had two outs.

Faith shot Alyssa a panicked look. "Okay, start biting your nails now."

The third batter came out. He walked slowly to the batter's box, his shoulders bunched up. The whole inning, maybe even the game, rested on those shoulders—Alyssa hoped he could handle it. He was their only freshman starter, and he hadn't had a hit all day.

The first pitch was another of those beautiful fastballs. The rookie watched it pass, nodded, and crowded the plate.

"What's he doing?" Faith asked.

Alyssa felt a smile coming on. "Proving why he made varsity at fourteen."

The next pitch was another curve, slightly outside. By moving in, the batter had given himself enough reach to pick it up. The ball pinged off his bat, flew over the shortstop's head, and dropped into the grass ten yards away from the center fielder. With that little, unassuming hit, the third batter had a single.

Alyssa let out a long breath. "Tristan's coming out."

He was all business as he swaggered to the plate. If he was worried about being on the hook, he didn't show it. He'd only flied out once the whole game. The odds of him going four for five were slim, but Alyssa believed in baseball magic, and she felt like he was due for some.

He stepped into the batter's box, and the crowd hushed. Not even Reagan's fans were trying to yell and psych him out. The first pitch came—another fastball. Predictable, but when you had the stuff, effective.

Tristan swung, missed.

"Strike!"

The pitcher cocked his head, watching the signals from the catcher, shaking off all of them one by one. Finally, he nodded and wound up.

Another fastball.

Now that was different, but Tristan was ready. Time seemed to slow down. Alyssa saw the slight hitch in Tristan's movement as he adjusted his swing. His torso twisted powerfully as the bat came swinging around.

Ting!

Tristan dropped the bat and took off for first, not even looking to see where the ball went. He was the only one, though. The center and left fielders were racing across the grass, waving and pointing. The center fielder jumped at the wall, making a wild grab, but the ball sailed into the bleachers, at least ten rows up.

"It's gone." Electricity tingled in Alyssa's fingertips. "It's gone!"

Tristan was still running when cheers erupted from the crowd. He slowed, bewildered, and looked at the third-base coach, who laughed and waved him around.

Alyssa couldn't breathe, couldn't think. Tears welled up in her eyes, but she didn't care, not at all. When Tristan rounded third, she waved both hands, and he grinned up at her before crossing home plate and being swallowed by a mob of bouncing Sentinels at the front of their dugout.

Kyle slapped Tristan on the back on his way to the plate. On the first pitch, he connected but ended up with an easy out on a fly ball to left.

Faith slumped. "Aw, shoot."

Alyssa stayed on her feet, though, watching Kyle jog back to the dugout for his glove. He'd had that ball. He'd had it and held back. She nodded, smiling. He'd let it go, for Tristan. "Your boyfriend is one hell of a guy, Faith. Don't be sad."

"Oh, I know." She gave Alyssa a side hug. "And what about Tristan? He really saved the day just now."

"Yeah, he did."

He'd been the hero, but all she cared about was how the specter of a batting slump was off his back for good.

Chapter Thirty-Six

TRISTAN

Tristan's ears were still ringing from the cheers when he ran to center field. He had no idea how he'd hit that ball, and all he could remember was thinking *slow down* and taking a half-second hesitation before swinging.

Alyssa had fixed him, in more ways than one.

"Big hitters coming up," Kyle called. "Keep an eye out."

Tristan nodded. The heart of Reagan's order was leading off, and Dylan was tired. He'd powered through, but he was past ninety pitches now, and his arm had to be hurting. That meant a few long balls were bound to fly their way.

Reagan's first batter came to the plate. Dylan was already rubbing his hand on his pant legs. Tristan eyed the batter warily and drifted a few steps back. So did everyone else, except first and third base.

The first pitch was a changeup, low and away, and Dylan paced the mound. Tristan wanted to tell him it would be okay, but Dylan wouldn't be able to hear him.

The second pitch was supposed to be a fastball, but it didn't clear Dylan's fingers the right way, so the ball slowed. The batter swung hard, and the ball hurtled into the left-field corner. Kyle ran as hard as he could, but the ball dropped before he made it, and the batter ran to second.

Dylan started pacing again. Their catcher came out to give him a pep talk. The first baseman wandered in, too. The ump only gave them a minute, though, before calling them back.

The next batter came out, strutting like it was Christmas morning and the world was his. Tristan had to stand there and watch Dylan unravel. The batter's smirk every time Dylan threw a ball made Tristan want to punch something, and when the guy walked, he did it mouthing off to the catcher and the first baseman.

Dylan had his back to home plate and was taking heaving breaths. Tristan pointed at him and mouthed, "You've got this."

Dylan nodded and turned around to face the next batter— Reagan's best. He was going to swing hard at everything, and probably connect. Tristan took another step back.

The first pitch, a changeup, managed to fool the batter, and he missed. That perked Dylan up a little, and he threw a fastball.

The batter hit it square, and the ball sailed out over center field. Tristan's field of vision narrowed. Three base runners. Trajectory looking to be inside the walls. Second baseman in his line of sight.

Tristan jumped and caught the ball. As soon as his feet touched the ground, he hurled it toward second base. The runner on first base sprinted toward second, but the second baseman caught the ball and tagged him out.

"Double play!" the announcer shouted.

Tristan, chest heaving, walked around a bit, ignoring the

cheers—and boos—from the stands. Great as a double play was, there was a man on third. If the next batter hit a homer, they would have to play another inning, and Dylan couldn't take it.

Dylan moved slowly on the mound. He looked like a guy past his limit. By this point, he probably had at least one blister, maybe two, so every pitch had to be agonizing. Tristan wished he could take on some of the pain for his friend, but all he could do was make sure nothing went past him.

The catcher threw Dylan a fresh ball, and he took his time examining it. The batter said something to the catcher, who punched his glove and signaled for a fastball.

Dylan nodded wearily and wound up. What were they thinking? Dylan didn't have a fastball left. Tristan centered himself, ready to run in whatever direction necessary.

Dylan wound up, threw, and the batter crushed the ball. It was headed between Tristan and Kyle, to a perfect spot that neither of them would be able to reach in time. Tristan pushed off, running at full speed, keeping one eye on the ball and one on Kyle so they didn't collide.

In a rush of adrenaline, Tristan realized he would make it to the ball first. He waved off Kyle, hoping, praying that he had it. The ball was coming down fast—three feet ahead of where he'd be.

Without thinking, Tristan threw himself out flat, stretching out his arm. When he felt the ball land in his glove near the tips of his fingers, he held on for dear life. The impact knocked the wind out of him, and he gasped for air even as he slid across the grass.

Cheers rang out throughout the stadium, then Kyle was there to help him up, grinning from ear to ear.

The ball was in Tristan's glove, and the game was over.

Chapter Thirty-Seven

ALYSSA

Alyssa and Faith shoved their way through the crowd down by the dugout wall. The team dogpiled Tristan as soon as he made it across the field, but Alyssa didn't miss the quick smile thrown her way before he disappeared under a sea of gray jerseys.

She couldn't believe it... No, wait, she could. Tristan was a fighter, just like she was.

Her phone buzzed in her pocket. She fished it out, her eyes never leaving the field. When the team started moving into the dugout, she finally looked at the message.

It was her dad.

Looks like they won it—that Tristan of yours saved the day, huh?

That Tristan of hers... Alyssa couldn't help it. She started grinning and couldn't stop. So what if people thought she was crazy? She was going to smile for weeks, no matter what.

A: *He sure did.*

Dad: *Seems he needed that good luck charm after all. I explained baseball superstition to your mother. She still doesn't get it, but you can't argue with results.*

A: *Thanks for letting me go to San Antonio.*

Dad: *Drive home safe.*

Alyssa agreed and put the phone back in her pocket. "They'll come back out for the awards ceremony, right?"

"They should." Faith pointed at the infield, where a small platform was being set up between the pitcher's mound and home plate. "They'll give our guys their trophy there."

"Excuse me."

Alyssa turned to find a guy, college-aged, standing behind her. He looked a lot like Tristan. Shorter and stockier, but the eyes and hair and nose were exactly the same. "Yes?"

He smiled, and she was convinced the guy was related—it was Tristan's exact smile. "I'm Keller, Tristan's brother. You must be Alyssa."

"I am." She glanced at Faith, surprised. "How…"

"Oh, he mentioned you when I came home last weekend." Keller winked. "And when I saw him jump the wall to kiss you, I was pretty sure you were the Alyssa he talked about."

Alyssa's face grew warm, and her heart fluttered. "He talked about me?"

"Definitely. Thanks for coming. He needs a cheering section." Keller glanced back at a couple a few rows up. The woman had Tristan's eyes, and the man was built almost exactly like him, except lankier. "Our parents don't really understand baseball. They're proud of him, but he needs more people who enjoy the game backing him up. I can tell you know your way around a ballpark."

"She does," Faith burst in. "She used to play softball. She was really good. And her dad owns a batting cage."

"Really?" Keller's face lit up. "That's awesome. I better go back, but I wanted to introduce myself."

He nodded to both of them and went up the stairs to his parents. When he arrived, he jerked his head in Alyssa's direction, and his mom clasped her hands to her chest and gave Alyssa a thorough looking over. She must've approved of what she saw, because she smiled and waved.

Alyssa smiled and waved back. "Should I go up there and say hi?"

"Nope." Faith tapped her arm. "Because here they come."

The team filed out of the dugout, heads held high. Alyssa whistled, and half their heads whirled in her direction. Kyle, laughing, moved over so Tristan could see her better.

Tristan pointed at her and patted a hand against his chest. She blew him a kiss.

And hoped she'd be able to give him a real one—or several—very soon.

Chapter Thirty-Eight

TRISTAN

Tristan woke up late Sunday morning. He hadn't gotten to see Alyssa for long before Coach herded him onto the bus grumbling about "hormones" and "I'm too old for this."

Tristan intended to change that, but first, he had some work to do. The celebration for winning state had been set for tonight, just like he'd hoped, and if the team was going to hijack the ceremony, he needed to make sure everyone knew the plan.

Still, breakfast sounded like a really good idea. He rolled from bed, thinking he'd shower, but all the aches and pains from the game demanded that he stretch first.

Okay, stretch, *then* shower, *then* eat, *then* save Swing Away.

That was a pretty hefty to-do list for a Sunday.

After he showered, he went downstairs to see if there was anything—edible—to eat. To his delight, bagels and cream cheese, donuts, and kolaches were laid out on platters on the table.

Mom looked up from her medical journal when he came in. "I decided you deserved better than just bagels this morning."

"I love you." He took his seat next to Keller and put one of everything on a plate. "Even if you can't cook."

She laughed. "I know. That's why we're going to start ordering from Blue Apron. I want to learn to cook, but if someone else preps the food first, maybe I won't be so awful."

Tristan bowed his head and folded his hands in front of him. "My prayers have been answered."

"Now, now, go easy on your mother. She got up earlier to do her rounds so she could have breakfast with us." Dad raised his coffee mug in her direction. "Repeat after me— 'thank you, Mom.'"

"Thank you, Mom," Keller and Tristan said in unison.

And Tristan *was* thankful. Maybe his parents didn't care much about baseball…but they cared about *him*, and that's what mattered.

He ate quickly, whispering plans to Keller, who agreed to help. "I'll set up an app. It won't take but a few hours, and we can collect donations that way. I'll send the link out to the girls."

"Cool. Thanks, man." Tristan stood and took his plate to the sink. "I'll see you tonight."

"You're leaving?" Mom asked. "I thought you'd take it easy today."

Tristan grinned at her. "I need to see about a girl."

"Alyssa." Mom nodded in approval. "I want to meet her properly. Arrange that, please."

"I will. I'll bring her by for dinner tomorrow." Tristan paused. "Um, is the Blue Apron stuff coming that soon? Because if we try to feed her meatloaf, I might not have a girlfriend anymore."

"We'll order pizza from Grimaldi's," Dad said, hiding a

laugh. "That should be acceptable."

"Thanks." Tristan looked at each of them in turn. "You're all awesome. I mean that."

Mom's eyes filled with tears, and Dad patted her hand. "You are, too, son. We'll be there tonight. We're proud of you."

Now he kind of understood why Mom was in tears. He blinked fast. "Thanks."

Determination and pride welled in his chest. His family had his back…and he had Alyssa's. It was time to prove it.

Alyssa cocked her head, a softball in her glove. Tristan tried to read her, but she had the best poker face of any pitcher he'd faced. He'd found it both exciting and a little funny that *this* was the way she wanted to spend the afternoon, but maybe batting practice was a turn-on for her.

"Hey, Kaplan, you gonna throw that ball or serve it tea?" He flashed her a smile. "I'm waiting here."

She raised a single eyebrow, wound up, and threw him a fastball. Tristan swung and hit a ground ball toward first. "That's three out of five. You owe me a kiss."

"I let you win, you know." She walked toward the batter's box, graceful and sure.

Man, he could stare at her all day and not have enough. "Good."

He dropped the bat and closed the last few steps. She wrapped her arms around his waist, pressing her chest against his. It was warm and breezy in the field behind Swing Away, but chills raced down his spine at the contrast between hard and soft. He didn't wait for her to kiss him but leaned down and pressed his lips firmly to hers.

Her fingers found their way under the hem of his shirt, and she ran a hand over his stomach and up to his chest. He put a hand on her hip and drew her closer. This was what he'd been waiting for, and the thought of a long, hot summer stretching out in front of him made him groan softly against her mouth.

She pulled away and smiled up at him. "Seems like you needed that."

He nibbled at her ear. "I did. I think I need more, though."

She shivered. "That can be arranged, but didn't you say you needed to be at the championship rally an hour early?"

He heaved a sigh. As much as he wanted to stay, drowning himself in Alyssa's lips, her hair, her skin…

Stop that train of thought, man, or you'll never get there. "Yeah, I better run. You'll be there, right?"

She laughed softly, brushing his hair off his forehead. "You've asked me that four times already. I wouldn't miss it. I'm riding over with Faith and Lauren."

"Okay, good." He gave her one last kiss. "See you there."

And with luck, he'd be able to hand her a big check at the end of the night.

"Are you sure Coach won't kick us off the team for this?"

Jackson fretted like an old woman sometimes, and Tristan gave him an annoyed look. "For the ninth time, he won't care. We just won state. We can dance around out there naked, and he'd barely bark at us."

"Naked," Kyle said. "That's pretty close to the truth."

Dylan whacked him on the shoulder. "As if *you* mind. Didn't you show up in Faith's backyard shirtless? Isn't that how she met you?"

Kyle turned pink. "Something like that."

"Men, it's time," Coach said, coming in from the locker room. "Enjoy this—it's a rare thing, and you'll remember it forever."

"So will all the girls in the stands," Dylan whispered. "The news went around the gossip chains like wildfire."

"Good." Tristan followed him up the dugout steps to applause. Coach was right—he'd remember this moment for the rest of his life.

As much as he enjoyed the attention, he started to fidget after the principal began his congratulatory speech. Kyle, as team captain, was supposed to go next, and then it was show time. He knew Alyssa was here, seated in the front row down the third-base line. Her parents were here, too. His mom had called Alyssa's mom to invite them, never asking Tristan why he wanted them to come. They'd know soon enough.

Finally, Principal Adams finished his speech and introduced Kyle, who took a deep breath and waved Tristan forward.

"Thanks for coming out tonight, everyone," Kyle said. "It's great to have so much support from the community, and we're honored to bring the trophy home to Suttonville." He paused while the crowd cheered. "But we're not only here tonight to celebrate bringing home the state championship. We're also here to support a great cause. There are a lot of locally owned businesses in Suttonville. Many of them sponsor our team and support us during the season. There's one in particular we want to showcase tonight. I'm going to turn it over to Tristan Murrell to tell you more."

"Thanks." Tristan took a breath, hoping his voice didn't shake. "Most of us grew up in batting cages around town. When there were rainouts or we needed to focus on hitting, we'd find one for practice. Swing Away is one of those places. It's been in Suttonville a long time, but it's on the verge of closing. Swing Away is special to us, so we'd like to hold a little fundraiser tonight in their honor."

Kyle took the mic back without asking. *What the hell was*

he doing? "And my grandfather, J. Sawyer, plans to match every dollar raised tonight...two for one. It's time we started supporting our town and the small businesses that add so much to Suttonville."

Tristan stared at him. Kyle's grandpa was going to match... at two for one? It took him a minute to remember he had more to say. "Uh, wow, thank you, Mr. Sawyer. Anyway, if you look at the scoreboard, you'll see instructions to download an app. On that app, you can choose a player's number and pledge a certain amount. For every home run your selected player hits over ten pitches, you'll pay your pledged amount." Tristan cleared his throat. *Here we go.* "And each player who has a total of a hundred dollars in pledges, or more, will bat shirtless."

The crowd went wild.

Chapter Thirty-Nine

ALYSSA

Alyssa's hands covered her mouth as tears stung the backs of her eyes. "What are they doing?"

"Saving Swing Away," Lauren said, giving her a side hug. "And I think you're going to enjoy this."

The crowd started to go wild around them—particularly the girls. All of them. She turned back to the field and almost choked.

All the baseball players had shucked their jerseys. All of them.

Tristan included.

Oh my God, that's a lot of half-naked guy out there. Alyssa blinked. Yep, they were still there, still half-naked. Holy shit, had all of them gotten that much money already?

And…half-naked Tristan. Warming up in the on-deck circle.

Her brain was going to explode. She reached for her phone to make a pledge.

"No bidding. You're the guest of honor, girl." Lauren took her phone and shoved binoculars into Alyssa's hands. "You know, in case you want a closer look."

Tristan had the microphone again. "As you can probably tell, we had a few early donations to ensure we had to strip, but that doesn't mean you should stop pledging. First up to bat, Dylan Dennings!"

Faith was frantically texting on her phone. "Twenty bucks a homer ought to do it. I've always wanted to watch Kyle play without a shirt on. This is a dream come true."

Lauren laughed. "You could've done that in his backyard!"

"But this way I help Swing Away." Faith's face was pink, and her eyes sparkled. "And this is the real deal. Not me pitching him ten-mile-an-hour softballs."

"Fair enough." Lauren pulled out her phone. "I think ten dollars per for Tristan. Sound good?"

"Yeah." Alyssa felt faint. "Whatever."

Dylan hit a home run, and everyone cheered. After his tenth pitch, Tristan said, "Time for Kyle Sawyer. I hope your wallets are open."

Kyle walked out to the batter's box, and the screams were deafening. Having already seen him shirtless, Alyssa was prepared, but Lauren was still beyond impressed. "*Damn*, girl. That's the best investment ever."

Faith was fanning herself with a program. "It never gets old."

While Alyssa could appreciate the scenery, she was more interested in Kyle's swing. It was nearly textbook perfect, both in power and follow-through. He homered six out of ten pitches. Sure they were mid-list fastballs straight down the middle, but still.

"That was the best hundred and twenty bucks I've ever spent." Faith's cheeks were bright pink. "Totally worth it."

One by one, the players on the varsity team took a turn.

By the time Kyle took the mic from Tristan and said, "Next up, Tristan Murrell," the guys had hit forty-six home runs.

Alyssa stood and leaned on the rail to watch. How had he pulled this off? There were nearly five hundred people here. And Kyle's grandfather matching the donations? She choked back a sob.

Tristan took his place at the plate, and, God almighty, did he look good. Not quite as muscular as Kyle, but lean and all hard angles. And those shoulders. She could dream a thousand dreams on those shoulders.

He looked her way and nodded. She mouthed, "Thank you," feeling like she might cry again. Then, smiling, "Slow. Down."

He laughed and gave her a thumbs-up.

The first pitch flew out, and Tristan swung. Alyssa watched the play of muscles in his shoulders, back, and arms as he crushed the ball, sending it way out into center field.

He hit three more homers, but before his last at-bat, Lauren took the binoculars and handed Alyssa a glove. "You'll need it."

"Why?"

Lauren nodded at Tristan. He smiled and pointed at Alyssa, Babe Ruth style. Was he serious? He nodded to her, and Alyssa put on the glove. "You might want to move."

"Eh, you'll catch it." Lauren sat back. "I trust you."

Faith scooted up a few rows. "I trust but verify."

"Good plan." Alyssa punched the glove a few times before holding it up for Tristan to see. He nodded to the coach at the pitching machine, and when it pitched the ball, Tristan tipped it foul.

It was a little off course, so Alyssa bolted out of her row and into the next. The ball arced down, right into her glove. She held it up, grinning.

The crowd loved it. To be honest, so did she.

When the cheers wound down, Tristan put on his jersey and stepped up to the mic. "Could the Kaplans join us on the field please?"

Alyssa gaped as her parents stood up behind home plate and made their way down to the field. Lauren gave her a little shove. "Go on. They want you down there, too."

Alyssa hopped over the wall and walked over. Her mother was wiping her eyes with a well-worn tissue, and Dad looked near tears, too. Alyssa took her dad's hand but only had eyes for Tristan. He held up a piece of paper.

"Thanks to your generosity," he told the crowd, "we've raised forty-eight hundred dollars. And with our match, that brings us to fourteen thousand, four hundred dollars total." Tristan handed the paper to Alyssa's dad and covered the mic. "Will that be enough?"

"More than." Dad cleared his throat. "I can't begin to thank you. I…don't even know how."

Tristan nodded. "There's one more thing." He uncovered the mic. "Also, Suttonville High and its feeder schools will be making Swing Away their official batting cage. We hope all the Little Leaguers here tonight do the same. It's a great facility."

Mom buried her face against Dad's shoulder. "I can't believe it. I can't believe it."

Alyssa left them to absorb the idea that Swing Away could stay open and went to Tristan. Not caring about the hundreds of people in the stands, she put her hands on his cheeks and pulled his face down for a kiss.

"You saved us," she whispered. "You're amazing. All of you."

"So are you." He tossed the mic to Kyle and smiled down at her. "What did you think of the show?"

She laughed. "I want another one. In private."

"That can be arranged."

Dad came over to shake Tristan's hand. "Thank you. It's

not every day I believe a young man is worth my daughter's time, but you exceed expectations."

"Thank you, sir. I'll do my best to continue that."

Mom and Dad went to talk to Kyle's grandfather, and Alyssa turned back to Tristan. "Want to get out of here?"

He smiled, and it sent electricity to her fingertips. "Definitely."

Alyssa walked into the house humming five minutes before curfew. Her parents were curled up on the couch, watching a movie. Two or three notebooks lay open on the coffee table.

Mom sat up and stretched. "Have a good time with Tristan?"

Alyssa bit back what she really wanted to say. They'd had more than a good time, something she planned to continue all summer long…and beyond that. "Yeah."

She started through the living room, thinking to check on Buddy, when Mom stopped her. "Honey, we have something to chat with you about."

"Oh?" Alyssa took a seat in the recliner. "What's going on?"

"Well," Dad said. "After looking at what needs to be fixed up, and with the nets already done, it looks like we're going to have about three thousand left over. So, we thought we'd pay you back. For your dancing money."

Alyssa's jaw went slack. "You're giving my money back? But I wanted it for Swing Away."

"I know, honey." Mom's smile was gentle and proud. "But *we* want you to follow your dream."

Alyssa had held it together all day, through the announcement of the fundraiser, to the moment Mr. Sawyer handed them one of those giant cardboard checks…even when her boyfriend had hit a foul ball to her in front of a cheering crowd. But this? No way.

She burst into tears and piled onto the couch with her family. Buddy came galloping in and jumped on top of them.

"I love you guys," Alyssa said, her voice muffled against her mom's sleeve.

"We love you too, Chickadee." Dad patted her arm. "But this doesn't mean you have tomorrow off. We're going to be really busy, and I need my best worker."

Alyssa wiped her nose and laughed. "I guess it's a good thing I turned down Top Sports, then."

"It is…and I'll be doing the same tomorrow." Dad sounded so relieved, and it was all Tristan's doing. He didn't know her family, not really, but he'd pulled everything together anyway.

"I think we should have some pie to celebrate," Mom said, rolling off the couch.

Alyssa rose to join her. "And now my day is perfect."

Epilogue

Watching Alyssa dance was swiftly becoming Tristan's favorite hobby. He'd spent the first two weeks of summer break hanging around the studio with Kyle, helping out, but mostly watching. Alyssa and Lauren had worked double time to catch Alyssa up for their tryouts.

Both of them were really good, but watching Alyssa move drove him insane. He could see why she was so good at softball—with this kind of grace and strength, she could dominate any sport. The fact that she'd funneled all that skill into dancing made it even better.

All their hard work had paid off.

The final recital from the Dallas Conservatory camp was held in the Majestic Theater, on the historic stage there. He'd thought it might be boring, but the joy on Alyssa's face as she whirled around the stage had held him captivated for over an hour. She moved with so much beauty, so much poise, it put any athlete he'd seen to shame.

Now he waited at the stage door with Kyle and Faith. He'd carted a bouquet of roses all over downtown Dallas for this moment, and he wanted to see Alyssa's expression the second she noticed.

Finally, the stage door opened, and a gaggle of ballerinas filtered out. Gaggle? Flock? Herd? There were a lot of dancers, so they must have some kind of team name. "That's a bunch of tulle."

"Oh, look at him." Faith smiled at him fondly. "He knows what tulle is. We're turning him into a real ballet fan."

Kyle laughed. "What's tulle again?"

Faith swatted his chest. "You know full well."

If those two didn't end up married, Tristan would quit believing in true love...and he wasn't ready to do that yet. Not when he had a shot at it himself.

A few minutes later, Alyssa and Lauren came outside, talking and hugging.

"You were amazing," Tristan said before Alyssa could say anything. "I brought you these."

Alyssa brightened at the roses, but she shoved them to one side and stepped in for a lingering kiss. "I wouldn't be here without you."

"That street runs two ways." He pressed his forehead to hers. "So, you feel like going somewhere, or are you worn out?"

"I'm up for anything." Her smile sent a shock wave through his veins. "What did you have in mind?"

"Did I mention my parents left for vacation this afternoon?" he asked, giving her a scorching smile.

"And that's our cue to leave," Kyle said, guiding Faith and Lauren toward the parking lot. "Later!"

Alyssa laughed, and her cheeks were pink in the glow of the light over the stage door. "So they're gone a few days, are they?"

"A week. Keller's 'watching' the house, but he went out with friends. Until tomorrow."

She bit her lip, her eyes considering all kinds of things. "Tristan Murrell, are you suggesting we spend the next few hours alone?"

"I am." His stomach did flips while she decided. When she nodded, looking shy, his pulse raced forward. "Let's grab some dinner first. You hungry?"

She took his arm. "Starving."

"Did I tell you Coach called? He made me and Dylan co-captains of the team next year."

Alyssa stopped, a huge smile spreading across her face. "Are you serious? I thought the whole shirtless derby thing had him a little annoyed."

"Eh, he knew our hearts were in the right place. He's been to Swing Away a few times to check it out. He likes what he sees. 'Old school,' he says—I think that's a compliment."

"It is!" She went up on tiptoe to kiss his cheek. "I'm proud of you."

"I'm proud of you, too." He looked to see if anyone was around before winding his arms around her waist and kissing her hard. "Let's go home."

She snuggled against him. "Let's. Because I have some ideas of what to do when we get there."

"You do?" He led her toward his car, dying to know what was going through her mind. "You'll have to tell me."

She kissed him one last time before taking off for the car. Looking over her shoulder, she said, "No, I'll have to show you."

Tristan ran after her.

Acknowledgments

I fell in love with this book the second my amazing editor, Heather Howland, asked, "What about a story about a failing batting cage and an outfielder with a swing problem?" Heck, yeah, I was going to write that. But I fell in love with the book even more as Alyssa and Tristan started to fill out the pages. I love all my characters, but these two really struck a chord.

As always, books need lots of nurturing to make it to publication, and I would like to heartily thank the following rock stars for all their help:

My editor, Heather Howland, for being able to pull ideas from thin air that resonate with me and make for great stories.

The team at Entangled Teen, for their tireless work in supporting every book they launch.

The 1990s-era Texas Rangers, for cementing my love of baseball on quiet summer nights on the porch with my dad, listening to staticky games over AM radio. And Pudge? Congrats on that Hall of Fame nod. I knew you were going to Cooperstown back when we were both twenty and you threw rockets at second base.

Which leads me to my dad. He raised a girl who loves books, baseball, and telling stories. I absolutely wouldn't be here without him.

Finally, I must thank my family. To my kids, it's really weird being the shortest person in the house, but amazing to watch you grow up. And to Ryan, you're my past, present, and future.

About the Author

Kendra C. Highley lives in north Texas with her husband and two children. She also serves as staff to four self-important and high-powered cats. This, according to the cats, is her most critical job. She believes in everyday magic, extraordinary love stories, and the restorative powers of dark chocolate.

Discover more of Entangled Teen Crush's books...

OPERATION PROM DATE
a novel by Cindi Madsen

Kate ships tons of fictional couples, but IRL her OTP is her and Mick, the hot quarterback she's crushed on since, like, forever. Since she's flirtationally challenged, she enlists Cooper Callihan, the guy who turned popular seemingly overnight but who used to be a good friend, to help her land Mick in time for prom. Cooper didn't know how addicting spending time with Kate would be, though, or how the more successful the Operation is, the more jealousy he experiences.

ALL LACED UP
a novel by Erin Fletcher

When hockey star Piece Miller and figure skater Lia Bailey are forced to teach a skating class together, Lia's not sure she'll survive the pressure of Nationals *and* Pierce's ego. But it turns out Pierce isn't arrogant at all. And they have a *lot* in common. Too bad he's falling for an anonymous girl online who gives him hockey tips...and he has no idea Lia and the girl are one in the same.

Winging It
a *Corrigan Falls Raiders* novel by Cate Cameron

Natalie West and Toby Cooper were best friends growing up, on and off the ice. But when Toby's hockey career took off, their friendship was left behind. Now Natalie has a crazy plan to land her crush—and she needs Toby's help to pull it off. When Nat asks Toby to be her fake boyfriend, he can't say no. But Natalie's all grown up now, and spending time with her stirs up a lot of feelings, old and new. Suddenly pretending to be interested in her isn't hard at all…if only she wanted him and not his enemy.

There's Something About Nik
a novel by Sara Hantz

Nik Gustafsson has a secret: He's the son of one of the most important families in Europe. And his posh, too-public life is suffocating him. When he gets the chance to attend boarding school in America, he decides to masquerade as an average student. Then he literally runs into Amber—and she hates him at first sight. It's exhilarating to be hated for who he is, not for his name. But the more he gets to know her, the worse he feels keeping secrets from her.

CPSIA information can be obtained
at www.ICGtesting.com
Printed in the USA
BVHW041819050622
638962BV00014BA/86

9 781682 814499